Glenn Martin (1950 -) grew up in Sydney, Australia. He lived in the hills on the far north coast of New South Wales for twenty years before coming back to Sydney. He is a commentator on human resources management, leadership, training and business ethics, as well as being an instructional designer and lecturer in human resources and ethics. His work has included management of organisations in the community sector, high school teaching, psychiatric nursing, community work, social research, and editing of professional publications. His other books include:

> *Human Values and Ethics in the Workplace*
> *The Little Book of Ethics*
> *The Ten Thousand Things: A story of the lived*
>   *experience of the I Ching*
> *Sustenance*
> *To the Bush and Back to Business*

See Glenn's website at www.glennmartin.com.au

The big story falls apart

Glenn Martin

Published 2013 by G.P. Martin Publishing
5 Gumnut Place Cherrybrook NSW 2126

Websites: www.glennmartin.com.au
            www.ethics.andvalues.com.au
Contact: glenn@glennmartin.com.au

National Library of Australia
Cataloguing-in-Publication entry
Author: Martin, Glenn
Title: The Big Story Falls Apart / Glenn Martin.
ISBN: 978-0-9804045-7-9 (paperback)
Subjects: Martin, Glenn.
                 Men - - Australia - -Biography.
                 Life-change events - - Australia.
Dewey Number: 920.71

Cover design by Timothy Van Martin www.vanmartin.com.au
Book layout by the author
Typeset in Bell MT 12 pt
Printed by Lulu.com

The great enterprise can never be exhausted.
In truth, each end is a new beginning.

I Ching, Hexagram 64: Wei Ji / Not yet crossing

Contents

Author's Foreword

All of my books are about values, both the non-fiction books and the "fictional" ones.

This book is the fourth I have written as a National Novel Writing Month (Nano Wrimo) project. There are only two rules in Nano Wrimo: write a novel of at least 50,000 words, and write it in one month (the thirty days of November). Each time I have done it I have brought nothing. It is a matter of turning up at the computer on the first of November and seeing what transpires.

It is the opposite of what I do most of the time. My other writing work is planned and constructed.

One way or another, all of my work is about values and ethics. Over time I have formulated a framework of ideas about ethics, based on five core human values, that I think is useful. It makes sense of experience for me and it frames my thinking about people and situations. This is theory, if you will.

But the framework rose out of my experiences, not just my reading and reflection, and at a certain point I knew I should talk about my experiences. At the beginning and at the end, life is story, not merely a suite of shining concepts. So, fortuitously, I entered the Nano Wrimo river, and once you enter, you can only keep swimming until you reach the other shore.

I told a story, and it put flesh on the bones of my ideas.

It has become deeper in my subsequent Nano Wrimo ventures. The first two times there were particular episodes whose story needed to be told. But the third time, no such convenient scaffold was offered. This time, once I had entered the story space, I came to learn that I had to make my own way forwards, without being able to see very far at all. The first two times, the whole story hovered above my head, just needing me to pay attention and pull it out of that cloud.

The third time I had to watch the ground in front of my feet. There was no distant marker in sight. Only when I had taken one step did the next step become clear. It was in that way that

I painted the whole picture, filling in pieces, exploring, holding a sense of what the whole picture might be.

And now, the fourth time, "the big story falls apart". In writing it, the theme was the one thing that was evident early on, by about Day 5. There was, to start with, the story of my disenchantment in my early adult years. I wanted to tell that story. It was the turbulent, iconoclastic time of the early seventies and I was embroiled.

As John Lennon said, "My role in society, or any artist's or poet's role, is to try and express what we all feel. Not as a preacher, not as a leader, but as a reflection of us all."

Understood. Accepted. So I was prepared to write the story of the big story that falls apart. But gradually, as I kept writing, I came to see that the story kept going. Indeed, it has kept going continuously, and I can understand my life in terms of my changing orientation towards the big story. What makes sense? What has value? It is the same questions, the same quest.

The issue of value (I read from Madeleine Grumet*), "summons us to consider the concrete, visceral, motivated interest we have in what goes on". It's not ideas on their own that are important, it's how they are enticed out of or wrested from our experience. Our understanding of, and our feeling for, life, are inherently embedded in our bodies, our surroundings, and our entanglements with people.

Madeleine says it this way: "Our stories are poorly insulated structures. All kinds of creatures creep in and find refuge under the eaves, building nests in the attics and basement cupboards."

And so you will find here. The big story fell apart, at moments and in places. The continuities failed. But there were threads, even as the threads unravelled, and there were little stories that continued to happen, and omen birds that sat in trees at night. I articulated those stories, I gathered them and carried them with me. This was my work.

Madeleine Grumet has this to say of this kind of work: "Although our work cannot control the future, it can help us to think about the meaning of our past. That, in effect, changes the past and then, necessarily, the future too, though not in ways we can describe or predict."

 Tell me there is method in this, because the days now seem to be singing and full of joy.

 Glenn Martin

 Cherrybrook, August 2013

* From a chapter in the book, *The paradigm dialog*, edited by Egon Guba (Sage, Newbury Park CA, 1990). Madeleine Grumet's chapter is called "Show-and-tell: A response to the value issue in alternative paradigms for inquiry", pp. 333-342. My line of inquiry is idiosyncratic and fed by the fortuitous. I spied this book at a book fair, and purchased it for three dollars. I have gleaned much from it, particularly Madeleine's chapter.

Part 1: Disintegration

This is safe space. No one comes here. It's not the country, but there is the anonymity of a suburb, streets and endless houses, each one looking different but only as permutations nuance a theme. When you arrive there is a long driveway, and a tall fence that seems to discourage intrusion.

That is where the writing room is, behind the wall, looking out onto the garden. You might think it would be easy, to gather thoughts here and write. I have certainly collected a bounty of the thoughts of others to prompt, remind and entice me to articulate my own story. The walls are lined high with books, the fruit of an eager questing for ideas and the experiences of others who have written.

Years. But nothing matters unless it comes, somehow, to matter. There need not be a story. Perhaps there have already been too many. Perhaps the problem is that we have forgotten the old stories.

But of course I don't believe this. I grew up on old stories, and they kept us in our place while we were growing up. There was the story of what your place was in life, what was acceptable, and what not to think about. I kept open the possibility of older stories that might be deeper and wiser, but I found only moments in poetry and occasional fantasy novels.

The stories are unwinding. The stories are contesting with each other, they are vociferous. But even as they contend, the stories are beginning to lack conviction in the telling. The stories come and go, and mostly, they go quickly. They are set aside and people go about their business, going to work, playing their part in the social fabric, filling up on television, suffering depression and taking valium.

Everything is okay, I say, reminding myself. Everything is exactly as it needs to be right now. Because everything evolves, or at least, it can – it has the capacity. Behind my fence I have planted a new lawn. At first there was bare soil, brown, and now it is an expanse of rich green, still somewhat patchy in parts, but bright, lush, verdant and deepening. The mystery of the alchemy of earth and water and sunshine. This is still a true story.

I know there is constant passage between order and disorder. There is loss and gain and they dissolve into each other in turn. When things fall apart we look again, for cause and alternative. Some of us direct our wrath at others. Some of us simply lose heart.

Where did this start? Always with a story. Being four, and my parents moving to a new home. We had lived in an old settled suburb, near to a busy road. The sound of cars was constant, it was a drone in the background, and the busy-ness was ever-present. On the street there was always someone walking, or a dog, or a conversation at a distance. In the new home there was silence and bush. We lived in a little, thin-walled cottage, rough-built, with bush all around and no neighbours close by. At night it got dark and the only sounds were night sounds, crickets in the summer, a bird. Stars twinkling.

Which meant that growing up was about this bush-filled space getting cleared and replaced with houses – stocked, you might say. It was enthusiastic, cheerful and relentless. When you are young you absorb such things, but part of you, a deeper, inarticulate part, may resist. That part of me was cringing.

Outwardly I played out social roles. Allotted. School, church, sport, scouting. Active, aligned, and with acquired competence. But growing up meant choices I was not ready for. And things fell apart. The leaders of the scouting group left, and we were left, disbanded. My father died one weekend without warning, in my final year of high school. Of course you carry on, you continue to do what's in front of you. You say, "There is still that".

I went to university and hated the course, but endured it even so for two years. So hard to extricate, so hard to say I was wrong, and harder still to decide what else I should do, and then believe in it. I chose again, and it was a desperate choice – I couldn't see a path to where I wanted to be, just a stop-gap measure. My second university had embraced the ferment of the time and decided that all roles should be subject to upheaval. My humble efforts to apply myself to my new choice of learning were overtaken by chaos.

I bailed out, and went inwards. A critic might say I was merely following the crowd. There was a host of others who were taking a similar path at the time. But I went my own way. All I was doing with others was swapping notes from time to time. There was no track and I hadn't chosen any leader. What prominent voices among the alternative people said, I listened to. There were left wing politicians, fundamentalist Christians, New Age astrologers, health disciples, organic gardeners and drug explorers. There was hope in the air, clashing with the outrage of the defenders of tradition and dosed with righteousness, lunacy and depression.

Noise, noise. Why do I tell this story? Because I am here, and one wonders how one got here from there. And just exactly where one is now. One wonders about that too, because that defines what direction one goes in from here.

*   *   *   *   *

Yes, there were pathways, and discontinuities. I am not interested in retracing all the steps. Some bridges just burn.

The story that you tell depends on how you want people to see you. You could tell a story of pain, or heroism, or cleverness, or stoic persistence. Yes, after long enough, I have experienced many things. What does it matter?

I went to the sacred mountain and I asked the tiger spirit, "What is the story I should tell now?"

And the tiger spirit said, "I will not tell you. But I will tell you this. After all the experience, and after all the stories that have already been told (and many of those will be forgotten and that is fine), the story that you tell should be a story of the Way. And I will tell you two things about the Way. It is like a mare that is strong and that runs boundlessly on the earth, not in arrogance but receptively. And the Way is an exercise in beauty, it is a celebration of grace."

*   *   *   *   *

Everyone, it seems, believes in stories now: "We all have a story". It is a central article of faith. What does it mean? Some people have a story which is just what they would like you to believe. Some people have a story and it is self-promoting, or grandiose or sentimental. Or, to you or to me, it is trivial. There is something patronising about it too, like you would say to a child: "What's your story?" And you expect it to be a little story, cute, naïve, innocent, sweet and often mistaken in some basic under-standing.

Stories rigidify. This, of course, is both a good thing and a bad thing. After I left the city, and found a small country town to live in, there was a man who told stories. One time, I heard old Tom tell the same story. What struck me was that the story was exactly the same, virtually word for word. He had obviously told this story over many years and it had solidified into this particular form of expression. The same aspects were noted, the same acts and reactions took place and the same conclusion was reached. Even the final expression on Tom's face was the same.

I wondered about this. I have told stories of incidents and episodes, and they have taken form and accent to suit the audience and the time. I wondered what was different about what he was doing and what I do. I think he had arrived at his lessons and saw his job as the patient delivery of those lessons to others. I'm sure I have been treading the same course, but my lessons are either more complicated or I am still in flux. The lessons are still arriv-ing and taking shape.

I'm also aware that a story is just one perspective and any story has a multitude of perspectives. But I'm happy to carry a perspective. You can't not be somebody in your own story. The reality is that you do something, for whatever reasons, even if you know it's imperfect at the time. We live in the material world, in real time. Fortunately we usually get the chance to do things many times, we are in effect practising, taking the next chance to get it right. There is an aesthetic to life.

*   *   *   *   *

The question is, how do you tell the story now, and what

does it mean now? I think the meaning changes. Old Tom, the storyteller, told his stories because time changed and he could see a world of experience disappearing out of reach. He told stories to bind us across time. What did I learn from him? That people, when he was young, responded to the world around them in the way that people do, which is to say, if we had been them, we would probably have acted the same. Or maybe we would act worse, and that is the point. So perhaps a particular story is a call that beckons us back to remember to be courageous, or keep our sense of humour, or not be gullible.

There were limits to Tom's stories. They were about wanting to value his experience, to make sense of it in a world that had changed. His stories were prefaced by statements about the context – this happened when there was no television, not even electricity, and it took two hours by cart to get to town, and you only went to town once a fortnight.

I said there were limits to Tom's stories. What did I mean? It was that all his stories came out of a constant perspective, which was the belief in a constant perspective that made sense of life. You might describe this as western, white, Christian society, a belief in progress combined with the value of decency. It seems necessary to add that I say this without criticism or sociological haughtiness, just to say that Tom lived inside this framework. The world to him was constituted thus.

I saw it differently. I have stories, sure. This is simply to say I have had experiences and I remember things, and I have observations to make about those experiences. I remember, for instance, the boy in fifth class who was a very angry child, I know not why, and one day when mild-mannered Mr James asked him to stop doing something, Billy exploded in wrath, shouting abuse at Mr James. This in our quiet, orderly and industrious room of forty boys. Mr James asked Billy to go to the principal, and he refused. And when Mr James came up the aisle to grasp him and take him, Billy picked up the compass on his desk and stabbed Mr James in the arm.

Mr James kept his composure, and bundled Billy out of the room. I don't know any more than this. I suppose Billy got the cane. I know the classroom went very quiet, and everyone was shocked. I felt sorry for Mr James, who had not done anything to attract such ire. I felt sorry for Billy, because something must have been going on in his life for him to explode like that, but I had no idea. I only knew my own family, I didn't know what other homes were like.

So this is a story. Our lives are made up of stories like this. Events that make more or less sense. There is obviously a lot going on that we don't know about, and we can gird ourselves by adopting defensive attitudes, or we can keep such incidents in the difficult space, the space where we allow that the reasons are beyond our ken, but if we knew, it would make sense.

But this is a story within a story. The big story, for me, was the falling apart of a way of life, the loss of belief in it. This threw everything into question, from going to church through to growing up and getting a job. This was the only story I was interested in, because the ending was outside of the boundaries; not just unpredictable, but as yet unfashioned. Even now it may be only just taking shape. It's still hard to tell. It may be nothing, it may be that things will just dissolve into a whimper.

What do you do when you think something is over? It's not as if there is One Right Thing To Do. Perhaps the thing to do is stay and argue, to try and work it out, to try harder. Sometimes it is just best to pack your bag as quickly as you can and leave. Other times it is even judicious to give in, to submit and go along. Every time you have to ask yourself, which time is this? Is it a fighting time, a submissive time, or a running time? Fight or flight? Or freeze?

*   *   *   *   *

Running. I packed and ran. Perhaps I did it badly, or untidily. Perhaps I would do it better this time around. The singer Nora Jones said, "I don't know much about leaving, but I know I should do it today". My first effort at leaving was when I left the city. This was not so badly done. I planned for weeks, looking for a suitable place to go, finishing up at my job, acquiring a reliable car, jettisoning things that would not be needed.

I went a long way away, to another state, another community, even another climate. I packed my books and study notes into boxes, not knowing when I would look at them again. I got a job teaching, and did that conscientiously, although without great gift for teaching. The town was a long way from what had been home, so that was a good thing.

But once people come into view, and they are no longer strangers, you have to ask yourself, in what way is this better or worse than where I was before? It was naïve, what I was doing. People had said, this will be like going back into the past, a conservative and belligerent past. But then, it was just somewhere else, a long way away. And I wanted to be a long way away from the city.

Living there, I found it crude and cruel. Local people were not cruel to each other, but they cut stern lines between themselves and outsiders, and being savage to outsiders and the unknown was their way of protecting what they had. There was a camaraderie among them, a mutual understanding, in their attacks on anyone who was seen as different.

At school the children were polite in a subdued way, as if they had already learned what it was not acceptable to be. There were no creative fires smouldering there, ready to burst into flame. Occasionally there was a hint of subversiveness, perhaps a book on esoteric Christianity that was passed from hand to hand without drawing attention. The dominant voices were brash, established in their power, while the tide below the surface was riddled with corruption.

I lasted eighteen months. If my departure from the city had been reasonably well-planned, there was a quality of haste about this departure. I am generally methodical, and in any case there was a house to sell this time, and a household of furniture to pack. Nevertheless, there was an undercurrent of urgency, to get out of there, and inevitably there were strands that were left untied. And a lack of explanation.

The pupils at school didn't understand why I was leaving, especially as it wasn't the end of the year. So, I make up an implausible reason, which is to say, I know you will know that this is not the real reason, but I can't tell you the real reason, and maybe it's not even clear to me. I just have to go, now.

I left behind pupils I still remember. The Aboriginal boy

who said to me, with a wry, mischievous smile, "You know, you're not bad for a white fella." Clive, the country boy who used to put a package on the side of the road and then hide in the cane field. When a car came and the driver thought, "It must be my lucky day", he would pull on the string he had tied to the parcel. While the driver was stopping his car, the parcel would disappear.

Sometimes, said Clive, the driver would see him and realise what was happening. And sometimes, he said, they would get angry and chase him. Clive was a good runner, but he thought it was disappointing that a person should get angry about a trick that was just funny, and also a little bit clever. I could see his point. But he was philosophical about these incidents. He was treating the exercise as a study in the propensities of adults for humour and humility.

There were also teachers I remember. Phillip, the American teacher who taught music, who initially refused the principal's request to conduct "God Save the Queen" at a school event. He explained that he didn't believe that the school should be playing the national anthem of England at its events. Phillip could be both calm and adamant, and the principal became extremely upset. His event, which would involve public dignitaries, was under threat, and his name would be subject to scorn.

The dynamics between people can be interesting. Who has what to gain or lose, and why do they think what they do? Phillip relented. He said an interesting thing to the principal. He said, "Is this important to you personally?" To his credit, the principal did not remonstrate or try to twist the situation around. He accepted the question at its simple face value. He said, quietly, "Yes." No defences.

Phillip said, "Then I will do it for you." What I found interesting about this part of the conversation, as Phillip related it to a private group of friends, was that he did not seem to be claiming a victory or giving a favour. It was an act of compassion. You could still ask why Phillip and the principal said what they did. I think Phillip was trying to get the principal to think about the sense of national identity that was being conveyed to the children of his school. The national anthem was under discussion at the time, and in another nine years it was replaced by "Advance Australia Fair".

I think Phillip was also trying to get the principal to see how a principal might have a responsibility to think about such things, and perhaps be brave and change some of the school's rituals and patterns of behaviour. Why did Phillip capitulate? Was he always going to give in? Was he just teasing the principal? I think not. I think Phillip decided that the small public gain of not playing "God Save the Queen" was not worth making the principal suffer in front of his peers when he was not ready to take a stand on the anthem.

We don't have to win all the battles today. We just have to know that the war will be won in the end. And think about the suffering that is caused along the way, or you may become just like the enemy that you despise. That's what I get from the incident.

It wasn't enough to keep me in this town. I was on my way. At this point, with a wife, two young girls, a car and a trailer. On a long road south.

*   *   *   *   *

Before we left, we went to visit another couple who were both teachers at the school. Also Americans, as I recall. They had bought a house and land out in the countryside, quite a few kilometres out of town, among trees, and with a large tropical garden. They were quiet, gentle people, softly spoken but, at the same time, of independent mind. They were treading their own path. They did not follow the crowd.

We did not know each other well. I was interested in what they were doing because this was my goal too – to have some land and a house and a garden in the bush. Although, I had already concluded that I didn't want it to be around this town. It was fiercely conservative and unfriendly towards anyone who was different. I thought there would be good grounds to be on your guard all the time if you lived here permanently. It had not been that long since I had seen the film *Easy Rider* and how it had pinpointed the syndrome of a community that was prepared to savagely annihilate any outsider it saw as a threat.

It was a sunny day. We drank tea and ate some food, and wandered around the garden. It was lovely, and lush. Then our

13

hosts offered us a smoke. In this suspicious town it was a real expression of trust to make such an offer. It meant that you were prepared to put your welfare in the hands of that person. I was touched. I understood the meaning. I accepted.

It was a beautiful afternoon, sitting on the verandah, walking around the garden, looking at the work they had done on the house. I was appreciative of them inviting us to see their home, their private space. I was happy.

On the drive home, my wife said to me, "You didn't talk at all. You were silent for ages." It was a criticism, uttered out of the social norm that when you go to see people you don't know very well, you should make polite conversation, otherwise you will be thought of as being rude. I understood what she was saying.

I realised that what she said was true, but I hadn't felt the necessity to speak. I had been happy, smiling, and I had felt close to everyone in the room. Now I wondered, had they thought about it differently? Did they think I was distant, aloof, in fact, rude? I was crestfallen, because I had had no doubts at the time, and now I was forced to wonder, and doubt.

But it was true, I was retreating from words. I felt I had spent the previous few years reading incessantly, and talking, discussing, arguing, pressing a point of view, and pretending to know things I wasn't really sure about. Now I was reading very little, and the time I had previously spent talking I now spent in my garden, learning how to grow vegetables. I did read the few books I had on organic gardening and homesteading skills. I read them carefully and followed the instructions. I experimented and learned how to do these practical things.

*　　*　　*　　*　　*

The road south led to a hinterland, an hour and a half from the coast. We travelled, camping at beaches and in forests along the way. We cooked food over fires and sat around the fire and ate with the children. At night the stars watched overhead. Such a mixture we are, humans. Turmoil and anxiety, bliss and peace and gratefulness, all mixed up together. Trying to be better, lashing out at others, expecting what we don't get, knowing that that is how it is for the other person too. Being sullen, angry, trivial, mean, and often not even knowing why, about any of it.

I wrote occasionally. Writing is like digging, digging down to see what is underneath. Reading things I have written across many years, I think I have shifted. I have found that the sorrow is not the bedrock. Below that there is a choice, to affirm all-that-is. Deeper still than sorrow, prior to its grasp.

We drove into the country, exploring the ends of valleys, deep among hills along rough dirt roads where in dry weather the dust stirred up into the air.

> The sun is at a sharper angle now.
> We have been moving since the first wedge of light.
> The wheels cut their tracks
> in the ruts like a plough,
> flinging stones, stinging
> red dust into momentary life.
>
> Five minutes after,
> the crust has reassembled,
> has forgotten: us tense and balancing
> over dirt as liquid as surf.
> The old synthesis: master,
> concrete-world creator, has crumbled.
> Smaller, travellers,
> we find ourselves
> in balance with the earth.

There were adventures and misadventures, places we stayed but did not find our rest. But I was not setting out to be a wanderer, I was looking for a place to make a home. We looked for community, and that didn't work out. After this fruitless questing, it was necessary to find a place alone. It was necessary to withdraw.

The house we found in a valley was a retreat, although I characterised it at the time as a fall-back position after the failure of the endeavour to be part of a community. The house had things we needed, in abundance: a well-built house, a big garage, electricity, water, a serviceable road to town, fences, forest, a cliff, a creek with fresh running water, a place to establish gardens.

This is what I have learned about retreat. It happens when there is a situation of conflict and lack of progress and you finally realise that no progress will occur, so you pull back and seclude yourself. You are not defeated; you are preparing for a better time. It is pleasing to the spirits. When you accept retreat, you can build your understanding, your power and your capacity to bring the situation to maturity.

I have learned: don't seek to impose yourself on the world. Be small, and adapt to whatever crosses your path. Put small people at a distance, but not through hatred. Your focus must be on renewing your sense of awe, on remembering the vastness of life, and the love that lies at the heart of all things.

"The greatest thing in the world is to learn how to be one's own self", observed Montaigne. This is not an easy thing to do. All the maps are useless. You must write your own course. As Van Morrison the singer averred on one of his early albums: *No guru, no method, no teacher.*

Sitting in the house one night, savouring the stillness, I pondered the way of words. I had been touching on truth, but clumsily. I had seen the trap of talking. I wrote:

> Inevitably he became a master.
> The words came like flash and flow, strike and smooth.
> He danced his words of unknowing.
> Then time came when
> the logic of words thrust like knives,
> beyond the supporting ground
> of his own life,
> and time balked, and time saw
> pain, joy, responsibilities
> he'd never known.
> Then silent the wordsman,
> but for random gathered thoughts
> like last squeezings of toothpaste.
> New stirrings of the heart
> now were needed.

There will have to have been losses:
cut off a branch
to start a new plant.
Time must wait, and want,
time must dig down
to discover levels of content.

Opinions will have to become cheap,
visions stand to one side,
and feelings make room for love.

In his heart there are mountains,
and valleys not yet cleared,
where tribes of primitives
build their complex routines
far from the civilization of love.

In that vast forest
paths wait to be cut;
self finally lost, he moves more lightly,
abandons his totems of fear
and begins the difficult task
of touching on truth.

There are six rules of retreat. The first rule is to know that
you are liable to get caught up in old plans and old promises. You
are poised at the threshold of retreat but hungry souls and angry
ghosts claw at you. Make the sacrifice, accept the hardship, do not
act. You are shielded.

The second rule is to retire inwardly, not just as outward
circumstance. Stay quiet and avoid guests. On our property in the
valley there was an old shed away off in a paddock, near to a gully.
It was small, the size of a four-person tent, with a rusting iron
roof and flimsy boards for walls. It was dignified with a doorway
but there was no door, and it had a fireplace where there had once
been a cast iron stove, but there was little left of the stove except
rusty parts.

Although it had not been inhabited for over thirty years, the dirt floor was curiously clear, as if it were ever waiting for its next occupant. It was surrounded by tall bracken fern, so tall that from a distance you could only just see that there was a shed there at all. I drove past it often on the tractor, when I was going up to the ridge to collect firewood. The shed sat quietly.

A young man whom I didn't know came to the house and asked me if he could stay in the shed for a couple of months. He was writing a book. I let him, and he stayed for several weeks, and I hardly saw him at all. I know nothing about his book. I don't know what it was about or whether he finished it. He was in retreat, and I wasn't about to disturb him unless he was interested in talking. I respect the second rule of retreat. Sometimes you don't have to know what is going on for a person, you just have to give them the space they want, to give them a chance to see into things.

The third rule of retreat is to persevere, because you may find that you are still entangled in a web of difficulties that you cannot get out of. You may even have to get others to help you, and with their help you can begin to put it all at a distance. The experience can be one of affliction that does not allow you to achieve great things. Think of this time as an offering to the spirits. You are still proceeding step by step, and you are in fact gathering energy.

The fourth rule is that you may be confronted by troublesome past experiences. You find the hidden sickness of your life as it has been up until now. Have an open heart and adopt the stance of correctness. Embrace goodness. I see this more clearly now. These times came. If I had had sufficient faith then, I would have known more clearly the times when it was good. But I struggled. I wanted to do so much, and I wanted so much to happen.

Now I think, "It is okay. It is already okay. It is always okay. Open your eyes."

What is the fifth rule? Inner regrouping lets your real purpose shine. Excellence through retiring. Though you may feel isolated and unsure, you have a profound connection to the spirits working at a great distance. You are a wanderer in spirit, and you make a connection in a single try. There is praise and a mandate. Whatever you do will be successful. There is no need to be afraid to act alone.

The sixth rule is about the richness that comes when you have emptied yourself out. To retreat is to treasure the emptiness, to strip yourself bare of all your presumption and pomposity. Inner stripping leads to a breakthrough. You bring wealth and fertility to everything around you. You may want to break out into eloquent speech (again), but do not forget the lessons of retreat. If you try to act prematurely you will be lost in the abyss. Start slowly and express the joy. You are doing exactly what is needed.

*　　*　　*　　*　　*

It was hard to do this. It was hard to stop. There is always so much to be done. Striving, striving. But I do remember times of peace. It was a few months after I had moved to the valley, still at this point with a wife and two children. The house was settled, rooms furnished, furnishings adequate, the area surrounding the house tamed, not so many snakes appearing around the house, and a garden had been dug.

Better yet, I had connected the spring water to a system of micro-sprinklers that covered the garden. Overnight the array of tiny sprinklers would water the entire garden softly. There was a sufficient flow of water from the header tank at the spring to last the night, then the tank would fill up again during the day. By morning the garden would be soaked, and the plants were thriving. I knew enough now about growing vegetables to be confident that seeds would sprout, to know when to transplant seedlings, how often I needed to weed, how much mulch to use, and how long it would be before I could pick a crop.

Yes, that felt good. There was strength in this. It was the fruit of retreat. When it came time for the local agricultural show I had several entries in the herbs and vegetables section. Tentatively, because I didn't know what the local culture was about these things. Perhaps Mr Smith had won the prize for the best carrots for the last twenty years, and I would start a grudge contest.

I won prizes. There were three Firsts and two Seconds, and I even received a comment of admiration from one old farmer. Me with my long hair and beard, he with his sunburned skin and

Akubra hat.

It wasn't just about the vegetables. It never is. It was about standing on my own ground, in my own way, even if this was a modest endeavour.

*　*　*　*　*

There was a shock. Without warning my wife left, taking the children with her. Being in this relationship had defined me for the last few years – being a husband, and being the father part of a family. The experience drained me, and it was some time before I recovered.

In the meantime I carried on, working, cooking and eating out of discipline rather than desire, sweeping the floor regularly, keeping the house tidy. I tended the garden still, giving vegetables away when they were in plenty.

After months, I resolved to return to living. The wanderer learns not to presume, not to depend on solidity, however solid it may seem. It came down to this: we wander best with simple rules – to enjoy, to act with correctness, to be bold but polite, and to know stillness in movement. It is grand.

I also tempered my disappointment about the failure of communities. I read this about Findhorn, the famed Scottish spiritual community, which was, of course, an experiment: "I think I had some expectations that this could be the 'ideal' place – which I haven't found it to be. However, I've learned that the answers aren't in a change of environment, they are in a change of consciousness."

All the truths sound so trite, like what one of the children at Findhorn said to a visitor about meditation: "You don't know what meditation is? You just close your eyes and be silent." Ah, yes, in fact, yes.

But more to the point is this analogy about what happens in a community. The community is like a labyrinth. When you first approach it, it looks as if you can walk straight in to the centre. But then you find you can't. Your path diverges to the side, and you find yourself following a path that sometimes heads directly away from the centre, and around, and back on itself, until you discover that you need to traverse every single part of the circle to get to the centre.

In the book I read about Findhorn, the writer comments on the labyrinth analogy: "In a similar way, we must integrate our insight with every aspect of human life before returning, finally, to the centre of our being". I did not find myself in a community, but the message applied nonetheless. What is set in motion by contemplating the self can result in a transformed life. Our life has to be brought into alignment with our changing consciousness.

It was much easier to say this, of course, than to point to specific aspects of my life that reflected change, much less spiritual change. But I did have my simple rules of wandering to guide me. They were mine. I had articulated them, and I followed them like a mare following its instinct across the wide plain. I have realised that it is just about practice, that is all. One has a practice that one does faithfully, regularly, and sets aside circumstance to keep on with the practice.

And I have standards of behaviour that I follow. I aim to adhere to integrity. I do not claim great powers, not anything exceptional at all. I claim only to practise.

I have walked a labyrinth. All this came later. I helped to organise a conference, and there was a labyrinth in the grounds of the venue, which we walked in our opening ceremony. Don't make too much of this. It was just a group of people, most of whom had not met each other before. We were just doing obeisance, offering our spirits in modesty to honour the time that we were to spend together.

I wrote this:

In the labyrinth I learned
the sound of feet,
I learned
to put one foot
in front of the other.
The next step
is all the path gives you.
And looking up,

the people you see
heading in the opposite direction
may in fact be further ahead or behind.
I learned
that you need
to walk every step of the labyrinth
in order to get to the centre.
I learned pace –
when sometimes at every breath
you have to turn direction again
and sometimes
you walk for ages –
long, striding steps
until rhythm is natural,
but knowing always
that the path will turn
and turn again
until we arrive at the still centre
where new life bubbles up out of
nothingness – *prima materia*
to which I bring flesh,
and words to mark the journey.

Not very far from the valley where I lived, there is a crystal place you can visit (yes, it is a place, not a palace). They have a large vision, they have invested in rescuing the world for spirit. They too have a labyrinth, a shady myriad of paths rimmed with small stones and moss and surrounded by trees. When you come to the beginning, you find a plaque affixed to a stone, and the Dalai Lama speaks to you from the plaque. He says, "There is only one religion the world needs, and that is the religion of kindness."

I cannot read this plaque without my eyes brimming with tears.

There is another labyrinth I have seen. It is a small thing but a thing of wonder. A girl at a Rudolf Steiner school took it on as a project, and the school gave her a space in the outskirts of the school grounds, in among the bush, past the playing area. Near to the city's harbour, a gifted place. So she gathered stones, and marked out the circle, with the help of her father, and made the paths leading to the centre.

Then she studied the history and significance of labyrinths, their spiritual meaning, and wrote it as an essay. A simple thing, although hard work. But perhaps that is it: the best thing to do at any time is a simple thing that is aimed at the source, our great arc from birth to wilderness and back again.

I read:

"The only thing we did that was wrong,
was to stay in the wilderness for too long."

Gradually, books were creeping back into my life. People would have a book about Findhorn, or a dog-eared copy of a book on home birthing or heart politics. Or a novel by Tom Robbins, Richard Brautigan, Kurt Vonnegut or Tom Wolfe. The books did the rounds, house to house over many months. And they accumulated, in a modest way, on shelves in my house.

They were the books of outsiders, people who seemed to despair of the mainstream and who wanted some small part of life, their own sphere, to be sane and kind and fun, and in harmony with the earth. I soaked in their stories, happy to see the world from their stance for a while. And then the experience faded and there was the world that was in front of me again.

It's hard to say what part a book plays. Brain researchers say it's hard to tell sometimes the difference between the brain's reactions to an event in the world and a simulated event like a book or a movie. The moral of this fact for some people is that we should subject our minds only to positive, uplifting experiences and sentiments.

Perhaps there is value in this view, but I suspect the truth is somewhat more subtle. Victor Frankl, who survived Auschwitz and wrote about it in *Man's Search for Meaning*, said it was the optimists who fell apart first. To survive, you needed a belief that sustained you in the midst of whatever was happening. For him, it was the notion that you meet life with the meaning that you bring to it, and what meaning you bring to it is your choice.

Jim Collins, who wrote a book on what makes companies

become successful called *Good to Great*, also has a story about a man surviving a prisoner of war experience. The man, a US soldier whose plane was shot down over North Vietnam during the war, said the same thing – the optimists fell apart first.

This soldier said you have to master two things simultaneously. First, you have to make a brutally honest assessment of the seriousness of your current situation, however bad that may be. Second, you have to have an absolute certainty that you will be alright in the end, whatever that may mean in the physical world.

I agree with Frankl and the soldier. When you hold these two thoughts simultaneously – unblinkered recognition of what is so in the material world at this point in time, and what is the best possible form of all-that-is – then you are connected to a creative force which may be called divine energy.

Perhaps my flight from the city and my attempts to find an alternative community were not essential, or even important in themselves. Perhaps all this was just a forum for delving into the broadest question, working out what is the most positive way to respond to the experiences that confront us, both personally and at society level.

It is the words that are difficult. It is easy enough to talk about the material world. We have science, and we have become very good at describing and explaining the material world. But in the psychological realm it is not so easy. We are riddled with presumption and assumptions. What we have identified over one hundred years is interesting but not definitive.

And to find language to talk about the realm of the possible, the essence, the spirit, it is difficult even to start. One person will want to say God, and another will object to that. One person will want to admit angels and supernatural beings, and some will be appalled at this fancifulness. They will want to anchor spirit in the energy of the universe, so that a scientist will eventually have to acknowledge it.

Going to live in the bush was not just a flight from the city and the crass way of life engendered by consumerism. It was a flight from books as well. I was after direct experience. I wanted to explore and enjoy the simple experiences of looking after a house, having a garden, and cooking food. I did not want to live

24

life second-hand, through reading about other people's experiences and digesting other people's thoughts.

This is not what I think now. In the house where I live now I have a large library, and ironically I have been accused of living my life through books. I didn't respond to this accusation when it was made. It was a bit like being shot with a tiny water pistol on a hot summer's day.

In my non-reading years (this is probably not literally true; I probably read quite a few books then, but it feels like it was a readingless period) the emphasis was on practical pursuits, on wanting to build a shed, a chook yard, to instal a better watering system from the spring, or landscape the area around the house. But the thoughts continued, churning along, and people came around and talked about things, cosmic as well as practical. Robert Pirsig had given us *Zen and the Art of Motor Cycle Maintenance* and Richard Bach had given us *Jonathan Livingston Seagull*. Here were new stories to prompt conversations.

It is not a question of choosing between living your life through books and "really living". There is a constant flow between experiences and thoughts, and books can be part of that conversation if you look at them that way. It's like what Victor Frankl said about the optimists – if you deny what's happening to you, you are headed for ruin. He was talking about escapism. Books can serve that purpose, true, but they can also do the opposite. They can challenge how you see the world. It depends on how open you choose to be.

*   *   *   *   *

When dark forces spread and the brightness is too high to reach, one should retreat rather than compromise with the darkness. This is the essence of retreat, to withdraw from strife that is too much for you to take on. You do not have the understanding or the capacity to deal with it. That is why there are rules for retreat. The most essential rule is to adhere to virtue. Stay modest and sober, honest and grateful, kind and decent.

Others will say you should let your hair down. Get drunk. You deserve it. Loosen up.

Ha! I would say. My advice is, breathe in, breathe out. Watch the surface of the pond. Let tears fall if they must, but don't hang onto them. In time, the surface of the pond will clear, and you will see, there is joy in the water. In time, you will feel the urge to move again. Then move.

How do you know when it is time to end your retreat? Certainly not when everything is worked out. Again, ha! I was simply aware of becoming restless, of wanting to do more. Money was a factor. It was becoming prudent to look for a job. In the time I lived in the valley, there were several phases of retreat. This is how it happened the first time.

I used to read the local paper, curious to see what was happening for people in the local area, what their lives were like. It is not very different anywhere, in the city or the country. There are business people, there are people who do public service, there are precocious children and there is sport. The journalists are more or less adept at English. People buy things and sell them, and then there are the job vacancies.

This was the scantiest part of the classifieds. One week there might be a shop assistant wanted, or a farm hand, or a low-level government job somewhere. I found my job in the paper, but not in the Positions Vacant column. For no reason that I have ever fathomed, it was in the Wanted column. I was reading the column because I was tuning into the local community and what was up for exchange between people.

Apparently there was a need for a mathematics teacher at a local Catholic high school. I read this sitting with a cup of tea on the verandah, looking at my flourishing garden. Now it wasn't out of the question that there were other people in the district who received the newspaper who also fitted the bill. But it did seem rather specific. I couldn't deny that I fitted this rather precise description.

Then there was the question of whether a religious high school would be at all interested in a long-haired young man who lived in the hills and who didn't belong to any church. Who had some little history of teaching, but who had dropped out of two degrees along the way.

I was accepted. Not in a casual way, as if it didn't really

matter to them, or grudgingly, as if they couldn't find anyone else willing, but accepted with respect and consideration. I had to think about the opposite factor then – were they hoping to convert me to the church? But I never felt any pressure to do that. My common ground was faith that life needs to be understood in terms of spirit, not just material matter, and that the well-lived life is characterised by ethics.

I could say, it was as if the principal, a nun, employed me in obedience to what needed to happen, not out of any personal preference or professional judgement. Or perhaps more correctly, that there was a convergence between her professional judgement and the recommendations of the universe.

There are other times I have come out of retreat with similar clarity. When I came back to the city, I had been looking for a job for months. I had taken off the strictures and accepted that I might have to move away from my home of twenty years, so I was looking readily at jobs in a wide area, around the region and in two cities. I had finished a degree (it had only taken me twenty-five years), and I thought that I would get a job in human resources.

I found it difficult. No one wants to consider employing someone who lives hundreds of kilometres away. Even if they seemed suitable, they might get homesick after three months and resign. In the end, I had applied for one hundred and forty-four jobs and been for thirteen interviews. For an ex-mathematics teacher, there was a neatness about the fact that it was the twelfth interview that got me a job, not the thirteenth. Twelve times twelve equals…. There was a completeness about the whole exercise.

But the point of interest is the job advertisement. I had been applying for a wide range of human resources and management positions, with all kinds of organisations. The advertisements had looked attractive enough. I had a good degree, and the jobs would all engage the knowledge and skills I had acquired through university and experience. Then, after having read hundreds of pages of job advertisements, I saw one for a writer/ editor. A publishing company wanted a full-time employee to write about human resources for a professional audience.

I had the instant thought: I don't want a job in human resources; I want a job writing about human resources. Seeing the advertisement brought home to me that I had wanted to be a writer, and earn my living as a writer, since I was a child. It was an idea I had put aside in high school, in search of more practical options. I had not wanted to be a journalist, and that seemed to be the end of that.

Seeing an advertisement for a writer, in the city, fixed the seal on my retreat. I was not only going to get a job, I was going to leave my home in the valley. And I was going back to the city I had left over twenty years ago, thinking I would never go back.

Coming out of retreat, then, can be clear enough. It is the time when this statement resonates with you: "You have contemplated long enough. Take action".

And that other observation echoed again – "The only thing we did that was wrong, was to stay in the wilderness for too long".

Which is to say, beware of the insinuations of inertia. It's nearly always easier to stay where you are, and there are times when that is not what you need to do. In my current home, in the city, I wrote this:

> We are wanderers
> despite the effort to be anchored in plans.
> We are chosen to be in moments
> we are unprepared for,
> just so, we can learn to appreciate
> that too, and that.
> The wanderer learns not to presume,
> not to depend on solidity,
> however solid it may seem.

Coming back to the city, I felt I had to explain myself. What was my story now? I had left in revolt. Was I now saying that everything was alright, or had I just given up, given in? I did not come back with any feelings of superiority, as someone who had figured out the perfect way to live. But nor did I come back with any feelings of deficit. The truth was, I did not know how I stood in relation to other people. I had lived in my own way for a long time, without the need to compare myself with others.

In my job, one of the topics I wrote about was vocational training, and there was a debate there about how to describe a person's ability to carry out the essential tasks of an occupation. When awarding qualifications, did you give students a grading – 40 out of 100 (fail), or 70 out of 100 (credit)? Or did you just answer the basic question – competent or not competent? Of course, depending on the marking, someone with 70 out of 100 might not be competent. And conversely, someone with 40 out of 100 might well be competent.

The one regime is focused on a person's performance in relation to a group of people; the other is focused (although only in an ideal world) on objective criteria. Just so, I had arrived at my own views about how I wanted to live – food and diet, how I spent my time, the kind of clothes I wore, what I did myself and what I got others (e.g. tradespeople) to do for me, and what I considered to be recreation.

When I had time to consider what other people said and did, it was clear I was comprehensively distinct. And when I thought about this fact, in many respects, what seemed distinctive was the very fact that I had thought about these things. I had not just accepted what everyone else did. This was good – I liked being me, and not just a socially approved instance of a quality. Of course, this meant I had to be unobtrusive on some occasions (No, I don't have an opinion on who is going to win the football this weekend).

So, what was my story? I can try to tell it, as if the reader were asking me.

What is your story?

I went to live in the country when I was a young man. I wanted to be far away from the city. The city made me claustrophobic and I wanted to see if I could establish a way of living close to the earth – simple and viable.

So what are you doing back in the city now?

Many reasons were important at the time, but not now. There is this, though. I had many jobs when I lived in the country, but I ran out of things to do that were interesting and available. I decided that I needed to have a job to earn income. I don't see myself as an entrepreneur or a farmer. I liked having a garden, but I didn't want to do that as a business. So I needed to come to the city for work.

Also, as I grew older, I became less attached to being in a particular place, or even the need to live in the country. For twenty years I lived in a house in a valley. I loved my place. I loved being inside that valley, and the sun would come over the ridge in the morning, and disappear across the other side in the evening. I loved the rush of the water in the creek when there was heavy rain. It would be thunderous and magnificent.

But perhaps there are other places I needed to be, and does it matter? It seems that I need to be in the city, but I carry my country home inside me. I am reminded of it all the time. This morning, after there had been a little rain in the night, there was the cry of a koel, a black bird with a long tail and a little fan at the end. Koels would sing around my country house after the rain, and the sound would carry up through the gully. Now when I hear one cry, I hear the sound of a gully suspended in that silence after rain, when raindrops hang from a million leaves, and all life is contained there.

That may explain how you can live in the city, but it doesn't explain why?

It was time for me to leave the valley. There were signs. Many people whom I had become close to in the early days had left, gone back to the city or to other places. New people had moved in, and I did not feel close to them. There were new trends. The area became a refuge for people who were hiding from things that had happened, or things they had done, in other places. One man was rumoured to have carried out armed robberies in a city. Another was rumoured to have been involved in a suspicious death. It may have been an accident, but there may also have been a gun involved.

A friend there told me she had been in town one day and seen someone she used to know in the city. She had sung out, "Hello" to him. But he had pretended not to know her and walked away. She had no doubt who it was, and was troubled. She did detect that there was a furtiveness about him, as if he did not want to be recognised. She had no idea of what he might have done to require this anonymity, even from a former friend.

You take notice of these things. Signs add up and become omens. It was time for me to go, even after so long, even when I might have decided I was there for life, and made the most of it.

That's a negative reason, which is fine, that's why you left, but is there a positive reason? You could have gone somewhere else, and not come back to the city.

You don't have to know all the reasons or the long-term plan, you just have to know the next step. When I left my house, I rented it to two ladies whose names were Clay and Burton. I had a friend in the city who looked for a house I could rent. He found one. The real estate agent's name was Clay Burton. Some people are aggressively negative about such coincidences. It's as if they think that life is toying with them, and they don't like to think that life has such a capacity. They feel much more comfortable with randomness and blind chance.

But I think that blind chance is just another way of saying "I don't know". There is something to be known, it's just that we are not the masters of it. We are the mare galloping across the plain, not the mind that knows all. It is passion that pours through our veins, not all-knowingness.

I accepted that the mind of the universe had touched this point and that point. It was confirming, yes: it is the appropriate thing at this time for you to move from there to here. So I moved back to the city with a strong sense of peace, not forlornness or despair.

So you can't say what the positive reason is why you moved back to the city, or what the purpose was/is?

There were reasons that were important at the time. That was enough. It was a step made in the belief that if I were to do what I needed to do, what virtue required of me, then I would be taken care of. And so it has been. As the self is aligned with peace, so the external world becomes more aligned with peace. One tunes in to it.

In the end it is as if one were riding an elephant, sitting up there and being carried in a garlanded gondolier, like a man who is suddenly being feted by crowds, in a great colourful procession where the music is loud and jangling, and gaily dressed men and women are frolicking along beside the solemn beast.

I have to ask, what do you mean by that? Did you just answer the question?

Let me come at it differently. We crave words that make sense of all of life. We want to wrap it up and say words that are convincing to a crowd. We want simple truths that can be reduced to slogans that can galvanise us when we are sullen and losing faith. Yet I have seen people dance when all seems to be lost. Why is this?

Because part of them knows that the loss and the despair are fabricated. We come from bliss and part of us has never left. The body sometimes knows this better than the mind. I have seen this through music. I think I learn slowly, and some things have taken many years. Perhaps there are other people who learn more quickly. They might be the ones who don't stay in the wilderness so long.

I stayed away a long time. I had to take my own time. I had to allow things to settle. It took years for my old skin to strip away. When I lived in the valley, often in spring I would go up to the old sheds and find the skin of a snake that had now gone on its way glistening and new. Snakes have their seasons. Humans have to make their seasons by resting into the way of the universe. All that time, all those years, perhaps that is all I was doing, gradually unwinding, and learning that it was all okay.

Have I answered the question?

Why did you move back to the city? How do you justify that?

Once I learned that living in the country doesn't make you okay, and that you can be okay anywhere, it didn't matter whether I lived in the country or the city. So I could listen to what I will call the spirit, and be attentive to the idea of where it was best for me to be.

So you are listening to the voice of a spirit?

No, I am weary when you say that. I am listening. I am listening to all. It is spirit.

Is there a purpose in your returning to the city? That is what I am trying to get at.

There are purposes afoot, I am sure. But I don't see them in terms of a pre-determined destiny. I think life is more fluid,

32

and may be influenced by our openness to the currents around us. The currents are our thoughts, our dreams, fears, love, calmness, clear thinking. We can be repressed by dark thoughts, our own and society's. We can offer kindness and joy. And we can offer these things out of hope and strength, or we can be too tentative to make much of a difference.

So the purpose would be to articulate the message that we can start again, we can start now. We can honour the earth and each other and be glad. Mind you, some of us have a lot to give up. Many of us have heavy investments in lies and delusions. To come to ground would be to recognise that we have left the ground a long way away. It would be like experiencing ourselves five kilometres up in the air with a parachute that is made of ludicrous investments.

I can't tell people how to fall. I can only say there is a lot of love in the universe.

Purposes are important, but how we live may be more important, namely, whether we live ethically and in integrity. I wrote this, about my vision of the wise man (or woman):

> In danger his only protection
> is his sincerity;
> with confidence he approaches the disturbance,
> fulfilling what is necessary
> and retreating.
> When he is not in demand
> he returns to his home;
> if you ask him what he does there
> it will not seem important.
> Perhaps he watches the birds
> or puts straw on his garden.
>
> You will hear the sage in hard times —
> he is sharpened by adversity.
> In victory he will storm through,
> flanked, it would seem,
> by a dragon horde,
> intent on the last crushing blow.

But at once he will turn aside,
and pick his way back silently,
knowing sadness too in that hour.

And one knows
it is only the lesser man
who would stay to mock and plunder.

I remember a documentary on an Aboriginal elder. He was sitting on the verandah of his house in the desert. The interviewer asked him what he did. Mind you, to the casual observer, he was just sitting on the verandah. But he answered, "I am taking care of this country". So what was his purpose? Sitting on the verandah? Or taking care of the country? And if the latter, how was he doing this? Certainly in no discernible sense. And there lies the mystery. Finally, our ordinary senses desert us.

Watching the documentary, I had the strong sense that the man meant what he said. Perhaps our vision has to be this large too. If you ask the sage what he does, it will not seem important. Perhaps he watches the birds, or puts straw on his garden. But you sense that he has the strength of dragons.

*   *   *   *   *

I sense the question: what is your story now? I am only trying to answer it still. When I left the city, my aim was to go as far away as possible, to make a home in the bush that was self-sufficient, and leave everything behind, even the learning. The city represented filth and ugliness, grasping and greed, tastelessness and trivialisation. And I believed it was heading for doom.

Gradually I re-engaged, entering into relationship with the local community. I became less extreme and allowed my fears about doom to recede. I learned to operate on the basis that one had to do what one should do, today, and not on the basis of beliefs about the future. I could live modestly and yet be part of the community. I decided that being in relationship with society was more important than maintaining some supposed purity in isolation. As Martin Buber said, we are only alive when we are in relationship with the Other.

You might say it was ironic that in taking on the leadership of a community organisation, I became embroiled in a long saga of unseemly behaviour, from embezzlement to vicious politics, with people with disabilities as the victims. It involved a whole cast of supposedly respectable people – corporate executives, accountants, a bank manager, a solicitor, a doctor, an insurance agent, a local government councillor, a school teacher, a community health executive. Lots of people, all either orchestrating the crimes and the damage or being complicit or being too blind to see or too passive and weak to stand up and say it had to stop.

I was unable to prevent all this. It was like living in the midst of lemmings, except that I was pushed along in front of them and went over the cliff first. I was sacked and besmirched. I had no way of explaining what had been happening, and the nasty ones did their best to put the blame on me for the debacle that the organisation became. It was as if the town couldn't stand success. It had to be spoiled.

Or was it? Was it really a story of how executives came from the big city and wrecked a good success story in a small country town in order to serve their own political ends in the city? And by the way, they made a considerable amount of money out of it, although not as much as they had hoped for. If this was the real story, then all those local people were just hapless bit actors in a drama they didn't understand. The local ones who were crooks and thugs were just convenient as a mask to disguise the main plot, if that were needed.

This was a long time ago. All those people have disappeared. If you went back to that country town now you would not find them. Even the ones from the city disappeared over the next few years. I only heard about one of them years later, strangely enough, soon after I had returned to the city. He was in the newspaper, shown as a foolish and forlorn figure, loading boxes of papers into the boot of his car for a court case that was going to justify his delusions.

This had been going on for years. He and his cronies had been stealing money from the branch organisations to bolster their own dreams of empire, and now the money had run out and he was trying to claim money from another branch, in a last lunge for funds. But power had shifted. Whereas I had had no power to resist, this time it was he and his central office that had become the powerless ones. His court case was never going to happen, and if it did, he was never going to win it.

This was the man who had said to me after my sacking, "No hard feelings, but business is business". The chairman from the central office in the city. He had not planned to say anything to me, but it was in the midst of the jostling fury of a public meeting, when he was attempting to make his way out of the room as quickly as possible, and he happened to come close to me. So it was the moment when it was confirmed to me, from his own mouth, that his sacking of me was a deliberate, cold and calculated political act.

The most important lesson of all this for me was that I had remained ethical and firm under pressure. I had also overcome my doubts, when some people were insinuating that I was not able to manage the organisation's operations. As it turned out, the ones doing the insinuating had an agenda, and their accusations were disingenuous. I could have lost faith in myself, but I got stronger as the situation became more intense.

It is better to hold to virtue than to operate by unethical practices. Not that I am a champion of martyrs. It would have been better had I been able to expose the crooks and thugs, and have them publicly humiliated and banished. There were moments when I should have spoken up, but at the time I thought that it was best to be quiet. I recognise those moments now and they were mistakes. But I didn't have any experience dealing with crooks who were able to tell lies deliberately and shamelessly. This was new territory for me.

This whole episode took time to play out, months, and it was hurtful. I felt betrayed, and yes, I had been betrayed. But I also recognised that I had to learn from it. What were my mistakes? What were the clues that I could have picked up on early, that would have enabled me to protect my interests and the organisation's interests better?

Books came to my aid. They turned up in dramatic ways. One night, about the time I was realising how treacherous some of the people in the organisation's hierarchy were, I had a dream about a snake. It was venomous, dangerous and virile. A couple of days later the family, as it was at the time, went to the beach. During the day we walked through the shopping centre and there was a second-hand book shop.

I went in, and was perusing the books, not with any definite ideas in mind, but looking sideways at all the spines, and I saw a title that attracted me: *People of the Lie*. When I pulled the book out, the picture on the cover was of a snake. The dream came back to me. This was what it had meant.

Scott Peck's book was challenging. It challenged the idea I had that you should trust people, because that creates an atmosphere of trust. He was saying that there are people who, quite deliberately, do not act on this basis. They are quite willing to lie, without any qualms at all, to achieve their purposes. He wasn't saying to adopt the same stance, but he was saying to be aware, and don't be naïve. This is just how the world is. The value of this lesson for me was huge. It was transformational. It was like growing up.

I hadn't wanted to think about such people existing, and I certainly hadn't wanted to think about how such people operated. But after reading Scott Peck's book I started to accept that I had to understand this thinking. And I was in another bookshop, just browsing before I had to go to a meeting, when I saw a book with a black cover: *The Art of War* by Sun Tzu. It seemed important to have it.

What I learned from Sun Tzu was how you go about winning a war, using every stratagem and artifice possible, and seeking to minimise the cost of winning. I struggled to square this with my conception of living ethically. Live by the sword, die by the sword. I recognised the value of what he wrote if you are facing a war and your purpose is to win a war. Lie, cheat, deceive, demoralise. Maintain tough discipline, and strike hard when you have the chance. He wasn't talking about war as a way of life, he was talking about war as a way of preserving a society.

When this is the situation, Sun Tzu says it is necessary to use all means possible. It's what I recognised in Winston Churchill, the ability to shut out all softer concerns and give all to winning the victory, and demand all from everyone on your side.

I did note Sun Tzu's observation that it is always better to try to win the war without any battle taking place, and that people have to be persuaded that your cause is just. I think these are the two aspects that have been conveniently ignored by those business people who have appropriated *The Art of War* for the cause of business so enthusiastically. I think those two observations might put rather a different slant on how you should do business. They exclude greed and qualify the zest for ruthlessness.

In the end you need people to believe in you and what you stand for. Would you want to do business with a company that said its sole purpose was to maximise its profits? What would they be offering you? They are in effect confessing that they would kill you and grind your bones to dust if it served their purpose. There is no constraint on their lust.

Of course they would protest, and say it is not so, or that they have been taken out of context. These are the same people who tell you that if something is not defined and measurable, then it is not done. So if they don't have a measure for their supposed moral constraint or finer purpose (such as offering good products and services to customers), you can guess that it doesn't have a high priority.

*   *   *   *   *

Books were becoming my companions again. They were stimulating my internal conversation. Perhaps that is why I came back to the city. There is more traffic in books in the city. There is more conversation about things. People in the country are generally concerned with replication and maintenance. They want this year's crop to fare well, just like last year's, or perhaps better. They want people to be constant in their conduct and even in their habits. They want the same stories to be told again and again.

I don't mind this. But I have to ask about the stories. What if they are just stories of an arbitrary point in time, with a flawed moral sensibility sitting behind them, offered up as something more, offered up as everything that matters? What then? There is nothing sacred about the past. The one story, the story of "our time" – when I was young this was something I felt had gone astray, had lost its connection with the way of the earth and of heaven.

This is how Ursula Le Guin described the world of Earthsea in her fantasy novels. People, without knowing or understanding why, had lost their connection with spirit. Either they sang the songs but forgot what they meant, or they forgot the words to the songs and their lives became drab. People lost hope and became meaner. Arguments increased and fights multiplied. Gardens became overgrown and rubbish piled up in streets.

It was like a spell. I think people and societies do fall under spells. And to free yourself from a spell you have to slow things right down and strip things right back. Go back to the simplest possible things. Give away glitter and fancy, flashiness and conceit. Give up speediness, the constant activity, the constant need to be high. To free yourself from a spell you have to accept what is given naturally – light and dark, air and water, warmth of sun, breathing and walking and rhythm and the fullness of silence. Sleep at night, song of birds at dawn. Laughter at simple things, laughter that shares rather than divides and destroys.

Kindness.

When I came out of the bush and joined society again, and taken a position in an organisation, I worked for it to become something that created joy and satisfaction in the lives of people who had been sold short for a long time. Yet it ended in irony. My personal rehabilitation plan ended in destruction caused by people's selfishness and lust for power. You could have said a bad spell had been cast over the community I had joined, that turned everything into dust.

But people choose. If you have no power, you at least have the power to say "No". No, I will not be part of this. No, I will not listen to you, because it sounds like lies and slander. No, I will not support your schemes, because they sound like scams.

I ended my association with that community thinking that communities make themselves what they are. There are communities where the prominent people depict themselves as being eminently respectable, when behind the scenes they are peddling corruption and looking after each other at the community's expense.

But at the same time, the rest of the community is content to accept the façade, the charade. They do not want to disturb the fabric by questioning. Why? Are they just as corrupt in their own lives? Are they afraid that everything will fall apart if the leaders are questioned? Do they think that, even with their faults, the current leaders are the only ones capable of leading the community?

Then so be it. Things will be as they are. But, despite people's best efforts, the songs still seem to be forgotten, and no matter how hard they try, the gardens are still overgrown. And they see this as inexplicable and unfair, as if the universe were punishing them.

The truth is, I came back to the city because I had no place anymore in the country. You might think that the valley would have been a refuge, even if the country town had become incongenial. But harder types of people had moved into the valley too, people who were escaping from troubles they had fomented elsewhere. They would do the same here. It was only a matter of time.

And even the visitors worsened. In my early days I was sitting in my lounge room at night, on a new moon, when I heard a noise outside. I went out, and it was a young man on a horse. It was pitch black outside, and the horse was entirely black, with a long black mane. It took a while before my eyes adjusted and I could see him. He was long-haired, dressed in hippie garb, loose-fitting shirt and shorts, barefoot, and he was riding bareback, with just a bridle. He had no light, of course. And he had just come down the mountain in the dark, lucky not to have had the horse trip and go over the cliff.

He wanted to go to the next valley. Which way should he go?, he asked me. I didn't think he should go anywhere on a pitch-black night with no light. If a car came, how would they see him? But in his quiet way he was determined to press on, so I pointed him in the right direction. Remarkable. His was a quest undertaken with modesty and quiet determination. I felt touched to be present.

Would an older, more sensible person find it ridiculous and needlessly dangerous? Probably. But I compare it to an adolescent getting blind drunk and then driving his car at high speed down the road. With three friends in the car, two of whom die when the

40

car rolls and hits a telegraph pole when he misses a bend in the road. Would I find anything in that episode redeeming? Give me the hippie.

On another day, in my later years in the valley, I was tending my garden when I heard a car roaring along the road, still some distance away. This was unusual. It was a winding dirt road beside the creek, that went up the end of the valley, about three kilometres past my house, and ended. Why would a car be speeding along this road on a sunny afternoon?

I saw the car when it passed my house. A combie van. He thundered across the bridge and somehow managed to veer off the road and crash into the bushes, being left perched above a three metre drop into the creek. I wandered down. I thought it was best to take my time. I couldn't see that any serious injuries would have been sustained. And anyone who was driving like that probably needed time to cool off, and I needed time to think.

By the time I got there, the man had managed to extract himself from the vehicle and was standing in the road, somewhat agitated. I said, "Good afternoon. Are you alright?" My two young boys were up in the yard, watching. I had told them to stay there.

It was obvious that the man was primed on drugs. I don't know what, I'm no expert. He was speedy, twitchy. I said, "Where were you going? This road doesn't go anywhere. It just goes up to the head of the creek and stops."

He was surprised. "Isn't this the road to the next town?"

"No."

Then he became more agitated. "I have to get there. How do I get out of this valley? Is there another way?"

There was another way, but not in his car. If you had a good four-wheel drive, you could get up over the mountain, the way the hippie had come down with his horse. But I wasn't about to say this to a guy who was crazy enough to try, and then we would have to rescue him and get his vehicle out.

"You have to go all the way back to the plains and turn off to the left."

This seemed to be a difficult concept for him to grasp. He had difficulty believing he had come the wrong way. But clearly he carried some anxiety about getting away. I suspected that he had a stash of drugs in the car and maybe the police were after him. In the meantime, his car wasn't going anywhere. It was on an incline down in the bushes.

After he had settled down a bit, and realised that he would have to get his car out and turn around and go all the way back, he asked, "Can you help me get my car out? Do you have a tractor?"

I said, "No, I don't have a tractor, and my car is only small, so it wouldn't be able to pull you out." I paused, as if thinking about this problem. I thought, if there is something happening behind him, like police in pursuit, I'd like to give that a little more time to happen. But then again, I didn't want him leaping to desperate solutions.

Finally, I said, "I think my neighbour is home, and he has a four-wheel drive and a cable. I'll see if he's home. Just wait here." I didn't want him coming up to the house, and I wanted to talk to Max. I walked up to the house and rang Max. Max had heard the car, and his hypotheses were about the same as mine. I said to Max that I just wanted this guy out of the valley, so could he come down? He said he would.

In a little while Max turned up. Our visitor was still quite agitated. He wanted to get on his way. He was urging Max on. But Max was the one who had taught me the benefits of slowing things down. He took his own time to size things up, and decide what he was prepared to do. In the end he agreed to hook his cable up to the combie van and pull the vehicle back onto the road.

So the crazy man got into his car and guided it as Max's four-wheel drive pulled. The combie van came back onto the road, but then crazy guy had trouble getting it started. It was a dodgy moment, because I hadn't figured out what the scenario might be if the car didn't start. Just how crazy was the guy? Crazy enough to…? Well, eventually the car started, and the guy turned it around and started back to town. He stopped as he passed me and said, "Hey man, huge thanks. Have a good day."

Max stopped when he got back to me in his car and we discussed it. He said, "There was a moment there when I thought, if he wanted to, he could decide to assault me and steal my car. It would certainly be more reliable than his."

I hadn't thought of this as a possibility, and I felt guilty that I had put Max in that position. He was quite a few years older than me, although he was robust, not fragile. But he seemed calm enough. He said, "I'm going home to have a cup of tea, and ring the police."

Max listens to the radio much of the day. The next morning he rang me to say there had been an item on the local news about our man. The police had set up a road block for him yesterday afternoon, and he had tried to ram the police cars. Again the combie had ended up in the bush. He was arrested for various vehicle and drugs charges.

He duly appeared in court and was put on a good behaviour bond. In the same week, I saw a classified advertisement in the local paper. Our young man was announcing his joyous engagement to a young woman. There was love in the air and they were to be married. His name was Matthew. It means "gift of God". Something to consider.

There were many reasons why I left the valley. After this episode, which had its humour (and the two boys didn't stop talking about it for days), I felt that the valley had lost its status as a sanctuary. It was too vulnerable to invasion. In that respect, it had no advantage over being in the city.

* * * * *

But I mentioned irony. Yes, it might be seen as ironic that I came back from my retreat enough to engage with an organisation, and then it turned out to be an experience of crookedness and thuggery. Wouldn't the obvious conclusion be to reject any further involvement with society? To tend my garden and nurse my wounds?

Why would I decide, after all that, to step even further back, into the city itself?

"The only thing we did that was wrong,
was to stay in the wilderness for too long."

I want to make this clear: that the valley was not the wilderness. I was at home there. I still make the mistake of referring to it as home, when I don't own it anymore, I haven't lived there for fifteen years and I haven't been there for several years. The wilderness was being in exile from the conversation of society, not reading, not writing, not talking with others.

So, no, coming back to the city after the disaster of the organisational leadership experience was not irony. In fact, it was that experience that needed to be articulated for the city. Everything that happened there was illuminating. It didn't matter that it was a small town, a long way away. That just made it a microcosm, something of manageable size where fundamental principles could be seen more clearly. Why do people act unethically? What motivates them? What can you do about it? Is it worth trying to live ethically? Is there any joy in that?

I contemplate what nourishes people. I contemplate what I am nourishing. I take the corruption of the past and I devour it, like a tiger. Ordeals transform the soul. The shocks I have felt are the shocks of inner illumination. The channels are clear and the spirit flows. I expand and sense an awareness of the whole.

I left the city with the sense that its story was falling apart. When I came back, I was not sure how things had changed. Some things had changed utterly, some things had evolved, some nicely and some horribly, and some things had not changed at all, they were exactly the same as they had been, as if time had not moved at all. But I had changed, I had lived through "Shake", the thunder and lightning that frightens people for miles around. And I had learned to hold the sacred cup still, to not let fall a single drop of the dark wine from the chalice.

The bright omens emerge from the Ghost River. What is it I have to say? "We may begin again. What nourishes you? What nourishes me? Devour the corruption of the past. Make space for spirit. It is what sustains you, after all."

$$* \quad * \quad * \quad * \quad *$$

In some ways it was like coming full circle. I had been born in the city and I had grown up there. I had gone away as a young adult, for a long time, thinking that I would never come back. And here I was, in the city again. But not quite the same. I would not go back to live in the same area. I wanted to be close to the bush, among hills, not in the great suburban flatlands where I grew up.

And I did not want to be among the ghosts of younger days, as if I were fitting straight back into a former self. I was not part of that picture anymore. It was alright to make these distinctions.

I could say, I knew who I was now, and I didn't then. I could say, I didn't want to be mistaken for a former self. But I know all the flaws of this assertion too. Of course I am the same person. This morning I was reminded. A dove cooed outside in the trees, as it does on many mornings. I was reminded that this was probably the first bird song I ever remember hearing. When I was a child there were doves around where we lived, and they cooed nearly every morning, early, while I was still lying in bed.

So, I try not to make too much of being someone different. There are different aspects of life and living that I am aware of, that is all. I am more aware of and confident about who I am.

It wasn't that easy to complete the circle. I came to the city in an unhappy relationship, and it was some time before that resolved itself. Eventually I was free of it. The night she went, my son and I just sat in the lounge room and enjoyed a great feeling of relief. I realised how much those years had cost me. And him.

Yet happiness is within. There is external circumstance and there is the self we choose to bring to it. I don't count on external circumstance to make me happy. At a music festival I heard someone sing a song called, "Happiness is the road, not the destination". Cute words, but deep truth. If you are not happy now, what is it that will make the difference? And could you rely on that permanently?

I had thought about this when I came back to the city and the relationship was in dark days. If it is not external circumstance that creates happiness, then the conditions of happiness exist right now. And if so, then happiness exists now. All I have to do is be aware of it.

This didn't make the relationship any easier. Some people need to suck you into their angry dramas, and they hate it when you won't play along. They try harder. And you can't explain this either, because that makes them very angry.

When she was gone, and I sent her a message saying I was applying for a divorce, at first she sent long pages of handwritten bile, which I burned. Then she sent me a brief email message, just saying, "I suppose it was inevitable" (that we were heading for divorce). My reply was even briefer: "Yes".

*　　*　　*　　*　　*

The body and mind take time to catch up. It took me a while to get going. For a while I just cleaned up around the house, made it tidy and claimed it for peace and orderliness. I went to markets and wandered around. I started going to concerts and rediscovering music. Perhaps I just started to notice it, but bands that I had loved in my younger days were touring again. Even groups that had had brief fame and disappeared.

One day when I was driving to work I saw a poster on a telegraph pole for a group called Sebastian Hardy. It was surreal. They had been around thirty years ago, had had one album to my knowledge, then disappeared into oblivion. The album was a magnificent work, symphonic in structure, musically brilliant and emotionally eloquent. But there it was, they were together and they were going to play a concert.

I saw them twice in quick succession. It was wonderful, both times. The second time they were the opening act for a bigger band. They came on stage and simply played the album in full, the whole magnificent thing, with power and grace. It was so elevated above what you expect from an opening act that it left the audience speechless and in awe. When they had finished and the applause had died down, the person beside me said in wonder, "Wow! What was that? Who are they?"

It was rapturous. I think, you just have to accept such things and be grateful. I would probably never hear of that band again and it doesn't matter. What it meant was, there was something wonderful that I thought had gone forever, and it just turned up, as powerful and as heartfelt as ever. Tom Robbins, the author, once said "It's never too late to have a happy childhood." Well, not necessarily childhood, but life in general.

And this is one kind of story. The bigger story lies at a distance with a question mark suspended over it. It's the relationship between our small stories of day-to-day and the biggest-of-all story that tests our faith. Some would say that the big story is just made up of all the small stories we focus on. A happy life is made up of enjoying the pleasures of each day.

The other view is the ominous one that says we spend our lives rearranging the chairs on the deck of the Titanic, while all along we veer towards the iceberg. Or we are the farmer's chicken, and every day the farmer treats us generously, with plenty of wholesome grain. But all the time we enjoy the farmer's bounty, we are oblivious to the fact that we are getting fat and tasty.

There is another side. There is the Victor Frankl consciousness. To live as he lived is to live each day with the gratitude and kindness which is the meaning that you wish your life to express, as he transcended all the efforts of his captors to reduce his life to nothing.

In the midst of these different kinds of stories there is the story of poised doom, the one that says our civilisation is doomed because it is morally bankrupt and it is destroying the earth. In this story, we must all realise and repent before it is too late. We must change our lives radically and return to simplicity. What do I believe?

There is evidence. There are theories that see patterns in the evidence, and there are models that provide extrapolations from the past into the future. Icecaps and glaciers melt, unprecedented storms rage and floods and fires devastate. These things are not proof, but they must raise doubts. They could be signs. You would think it was a high-risk strategy to ignore these incidents when the thing at stake is the entire thing that enables us to keep on living, breathing and eating.

Yet that is also the very reason that business continues as usual. The problem is too vast and who will take charge? No one is in charge of everything. In this arena, mighty governments are just a bunch of children in a school yard, arguing about a cloud that has appeared overhead. It might be nothing, but if it is something, what could we do anyway? Maybe nothing we do will make a difference. Maybe anything we decide to do will be like the superstitious acts of natives in the face of unknown forces.

We have to observe the unusual for clues, and think about their significance. Things can change incrementally, almost imperceptibly, and they can change dramatically, and then people think that it has been instantaneous. I think of eggs hatching. When I lived in the valley we had chooks, and in springtime some of the chooks would sit on a batch of eggs. They would sit there every day, all day. Quietly and patiently. And I would check the eggs each day, to see that they were okay. And they would look the same, every day.

For twenty days those eggs would look the same. Then on the twenty-first day the eggs would start to crack, and quite soon little chickens would emerge, alive and chirping, with tiny beaks and feet and soft yellow downy feathers. It struck me that you didn't see any overt evidence of this the whole time it was happening. All that time, baby chickens were developing.

I thought this about the fall of the Berlin Wall in 1989. Suddenly masses of people were physically breaking down a wall that had stood over them for a generation. To me it was like those eggs cracking open. All the time up to that moment, something had been developing, and just now it was breaking out.

I think this about many types of change. Something is happening, but you may not be able to see it. So what do you do? Believe in the egg and look after the hen. (Yes, of course, with the proviso that you are sensible about the status of the egg. It will not hatch a chicken if there is no rooster in the yard.)

*　　*　　*　　*　　*

I don't pretend to know the whole story, to understand it all. I am no scientist, casting for truth. No, it is not the overarching story that I have, it is many small stories, that have misted up out of events and spoken of values that are worth living by. Stories show us exercising choices, and the choices speak of our struggles with values. The stories may encourage us or caution us.

When I first left the city I was persuaded by the warnings about impending doom, and when I settled in the valley I kept provisions at hand. It was a token gesture, because how long could one possibly survive in a blighted world, and would one want to? More than one writer had specified a date for oblivion, and I noted when these dates passed, and still we were all rushing towards this unrealised oblivion, not having yet arrived.

It was a time to take stock and think about things differently. It is not beyond belief that humanity could fashion its own demise. We have certainly been successful in turning vast areas of arable land on the planet into desert. Our political leaders have a responsibility to address the problems humanity has created. But I speak to people like me, who have to decide how to live their lives in any event, without the power to decree the behaviour of masses.

Seek to live an aesthetic life. This will not be a life of greed or violence, or sullenness or despair. It will be a life where you come back to centre continually and remember that every breath we take comes all the way from the first moment of everything-that-is. It is ancient wisdom that says, with every breath, the infinity of Heaven enters the finite space of Earth.

*   *   *   *   *

And then there is tiredness. It is one thing to affirm the positive, and another thing to live it. That is why talk is said to be cheap. That is why we live in a world full of promises and consumers pursue the novelty of the new. That is why the media loves heroes, even if it has to manufacture them. The fulfilment of promises is so much less obtainable than the making of promises.

There is defeat, adversity and damage, undeniably. There are no guarantees against these things, even if you live a good, clean and virtuous life. I heard of a Reiki master who got cancer and died. It seemed so wrong – the healer getting a disease himself and being unable to be healed. I have had friends who have died of cancer. The diets, the meditation, did not avert the outcome in their case, although I know also of people who have experienced the vanishing of the disease from their bodies.

Most of us have scars and damage of some kind, visible or within. I ask, how do I wish to live, in the light of everything that has gone before – after all that? I am interested in the stories we tell each other, and how one thought leads to another. Recently I told a new colleague of an experience I had had. The theme was community organisations, so I told of one of my experiences that was significant for me.

49

It was a hard experience. I remember it because it taught me significant things about the possibilities of humans, especially in groups, and it taught me about how to be more aware of what was going and how I might deal with it more constructively.

My colleague's reaction was, "You've had some tough experiences".

I felt I needed a sense of caution about my internal reaction to this. It would be so easy to feel sorry for myself, to make an episode like the one I told him a defining factor in my perceptions of my own life. And that wasn't the meaning of the story for me. Rather, it was that I had experienced something and derived value from it. In terms of the Victor Frankl perspective, I chose the meaning I wished to take from it.

After being sacked from the job I had held for six years, I did feel defeated. I hadn't done anything wrong or incompetent, so I had a strong sense of injustice. I was disappointed in that I hadn't been able to win out against the lies and deceit that were used in this power struggle. But there are lessons all around us about how we can deal with adversity constructively. Assume that our mind, or our soul, wants to heal itself and get on with life, and then consider how the body goes about this.

In that time when I was at home after losing my job, I thought about how the body heals itself. When we receive a wound, we experience shock, but almost immediately the body is working to bring itself back to wholeness. There is pain, but the body carries on bringing healing to the part of the body that is hurt. We can help this process with herbs and medicine, and rest and exercise in appropriate measure.

So I applied that philosophy to my recovery from the shock and suffering of the experiences with the community organisation. During this time of recovery, I asked myself where I should go from here. The choice could have been made out of a self-pitying or defeatist mindset, or out of an attitude that was more life-affirming. I could have decided to go back to teaching, with the thinking that I was safe there. I could have decided to immediately get another job as a manager with a community organisation, because that was where my recent experience was and it would be following the maxim of "getting back on the horse".

50

I did realise that what was important was the mental space in which I made the decision. There was nothing inherently wrong about any of these choices. It was a question of what each one meant to me, and whether I was making the choice out of defeatism or a positive outlook.

My decision was not to take a job, but to go to university and get a degree. When this idea occurred to me, it crystallised a desire that had been floating around for years. In fact it was twenty-five years since the last time I had dropped out of university, which was the second time I had dropped out of university – first out of engineering, then out of an Arts degree. I had thought about going back to university several times in recent years, but I had been too busy and, more to the point, I hadn't settled on something I wanted to do.

Now I knew what I would study, and it was obvious. I would take a business degree, and study what I had been doing in practice for the previous six years – management. It made instant sense, like finally figuring out which piece of furniture would fit perfectly in a particular space and bring it to life. My time studying was immensely enjoyable. Everything I studied I could relate to personally from my experience. They weren't just conceptual topics that fit logically together, but vital aspects of what a manager needed to understand, integrate and incorporate into practice.

Why was I doing this? I didn't know. It was just the next step, and I had no doubts that this was the next step. That was enough. I didn't seriously think I would go back to being a manager again. That had been for a purpose at the time. The future was going to take shape in a different way, which was as yet undisclosed. I have thought that it would be good to write a book called "The importance of not having a career plan". Life is what happens to you while you're busy making other plans, to quote John Lennon.

As it happened, the business degree was what brought me back to the city. The job writing about management was accessible to me because I had just finished a degree, and accordingly, could prove both my knowledge and the fact that I could write proficiently. So, that took care of external circumstance. The inner task continues unabated.

I brought my personal perspective to what I wrote for my audience of managers, human resources staff and trainers. This was a subtle quality, because the mainstream information reporting services for the company were intended to present and explain legal obligations and requirements, for accountants, solicitors and the like.

Human resources didn't quite fit into that paradigm. In human resources there were plenty of legal constraints that needed to be observed, but the curiosity was that in order to fulfil them, you had to exercise qualities of fairness and justice. It wasn't just a matter of complying with a specified set of actions, like making superannuation payments on behalf of employees at the rate of 9% of their salary.

No, the types of standards in human resources were different. For example, can you demonstrate that you have examined the risks of injury in the workplace and taken appropriate steps to ensure that injuries do not occur? Why did you not realise that an employee was being bullied by her colleagues? Did you provide training to all employees about the unacceptability of bullying, and did you ensure that consistent standards of behaviour were adhered to?

In other words, this was a different type of law. It required managers to go further than literal compliance, like keeping below the speed limit when you are driving. I think this distinction is glossed over. People – managers themselves, and writers on management – try their hardest to dress up all laws in the same garb, because it looks clearer, more authoritative and easier to enforce.

But the reality is that law in the human resources area is about what values you demonstrate. It's actually personal. Well, perhaps not entirely personal, because situations are considered and judged in tribunals and courtrooms, so the standards used are public standards about what a reasonable person in our society would consider to be fair, just and reasonable. In the unfair dismissal laws, the word "harsh" also comes under consideration. The point is that to be "legally compliant" in managing people you have to do more than adhere to specific rules; you have to have regard to the well-being of people.

It was a subtle thing I was doing, and I often felt it was too understated. Human resource managers seemed to derive much of their self-esteem from aligning themselves with power and authority. As a group they seemed to derive comfort from emphasising laws and policy. At their worst they were caricatures, with the proverbial clipboard roaming the workplace in search of infractions of the dress code. Theirs was a codified, legalistic and ultimately punitive understanding of the human resources role. Whereas the real need was to develop a sensibility in the organisation to the implications of being fair, just and reasonable, and to develop the capacity of managers, workers, systems and policies to have regard for the well-being of other people.

Yes, it is legitimate for companies in a capitalist society to pursue profits, but the law is there because, as a society, we insist on preventing gross violations of conduct by humans towards one another, in any context. That intent has not changed since the early 1800s when the Earl of Shaftesbury championed laws to restrict the employment of young children in factories.

I realise there are some who say it is no business of companies to be providing social services to employees. Companies are there to generate profits. But companies only exist at the behest of society and government. So, society and government say, if you wish to do business, you will do so in a way that does not grossly violate people. You will not be unfair, unreasonable or harsh (or cruel, or violent or destructive). You will have regard to people's well-being. You will take all reasonable steps to ensure that your employees do not get sick or injured at work.

Of course, a capitalist society is a strange place. You can't make people want to operate in this way. You can't make them listen to this message. Courts and tribunals impose fines on companies and directors, and they say, "We hope this will act as a deterrent against other companies and directors". Some other companies and directors use this as a lesson that they need to be more careful not to get caught.

My interest is not with those people. There are some people that you do not discuss ethics with, you just tell them what the law says and what the punishment is if they break the law. You tell them that courts and tribunals will not listen to their justifications with an attitude of tolerance.

I wonder more about the managers who would like to be fair and just and reasonable, but who find it difficult in their work environment. What if the competitive pressures on the business mean that you have to reduce staff numbers and require the remaining employees to work harder for the same pay? What if…. a myriad of other difficult circumstances that mean you have to be less than kind and gentle? What then?

I started reading about what makes a leader a good leader. I read writers like Joseph Badaracco, Warren Bennis and Robert Thomas, Bill George, Bruce Avolio and Fred Luthans, Richard Boyatzis and Annie McKee, and Peter Senge. Many of them talked about critical times in a person's experience when he/she had to make a decision of significance that would define them subsequently. And the issues were not usually about competence; they were about values. Badaracco talked about "defining moments"; Bennis and Thomas talked about "crucible moments"; George talked about "moments of truth".

At such moments, when you face a serious situation, you can realise that you have a choice to make right now, and you can bail out or decide to do what you believe is required of you. I know that that is what happened with me in the community organisation. I could see the corridor narrowing and I had the thought: "If you want to get out, you will have to go right now. Otherwise you must keep going, and do what it is you will be required to do." I decided to stay, and see it out.

This meant that I had to face the situation with the sum total of who I was at the time, with whatever skills and experience I had at that moment. I wish I could have done this with more lightness. At the time I was heavy with my burden, and the sense of injustice and of not being powerful enough. There was plenty of evidence to justify such a view. Now, however, I know that one's personal sense of inner confidence can be vast and palpable.

This is not fragile like ego. It is connected to the universe.

I have not had a teacher as such. I have not looked for one, and when I have encountered teachers I have not felt the urge to follow them. There was a popular saying some years ago, that festooned tee-shirts: "I surf alone". I could relate to that. But that

54

too can be a trap. It can become an expression of obstinacy and ego. I was not cultivating stubbornness, I was trying to listen to my inner self, which seemed to be saying, "This (that is, following this or that teacher) is not for you".

I have realised, however, that this is the function that books serve for me. I don't know why it took me so long to realise this. It's ironic – isn't this the very function that books were intended to perform, to extend the reach of a person's words? Yes, I know the response: with a live teacher, one has feedback on practice and performance.

What is the answer to this objection? To listen to some-one through a book, you have to read all of what the writer says carefully, so that you don't take one part out of context or out of proportion. You must engage with the whole of it. But there is an aspect of learning through books that may be different to having a teacher, and that is, you can read critically and selectively. The disciples of gurus are seldom encouraged to question what the guru says.

In my encounters with teachers and gurus, I seldom saw myself as an unquestioning disciple, and I seldom saw teachers who would have wanted to be questioned. Most of them had a platform and their purpose was to inculcate it in disciples. They would have seen questioning as an expression of ego, a mind that was not ready to submit and simply follow.

I would humbly suggest that there are teachers who have tender egos, despite the value that may reside in what they are saying. Eventually I decided to be content with my own path, which was to accept and accommodate what I resonated with, and leave be what didn't resonate with me.

I am getting to a point. I was given a book recently on leadership and Tibetan Buddhism, *Inner Peace, Global Impact*. It contained a passage about that inner sense of confidence that res-onated with me. In fact, I would say this: when you choose to live with awareness and an inquiring mind, such things will come to you and give you the answers to your questions. This is how you walk along the road. You have to be willing not to know your destination. You will only know what the next step is, and that it is good.

The passage was titled "Rousing unconditional confidence". Can you imagine anything more apt for what I was thinking about? The passage said this sense of unconditional confidence is the most important thing for leaders to develop. I read that carefully and I read it twice. Looking back on my experience I would say, "Yes, exactly!"

So what followed was of great interest. How do you rouse this sense? The writer called it *lungta*, meaning "windhorse". It involves tuning into your body, your emotions and mental state, fully acknowledging them and synchronising them, and letting go. In this way, the leader can learn to access the energy (or wind) of a situation and engage with it powerfully, as if riding a horse.

By practising this, the leader can develop strength and presence. The Tibetans call this "merit". There was more. The writer said there are four stages in the development of this quality. The first stage is meekness, although it is symbolised by the tiger. The tiger has its feet on the ground and moves deliberately, with mindfulness. It is content in the midst of life's unfolding. It knows who it is and what the reality of the situation is. It is not fooled or distracted by what it wishes might be the case. It does not minimise problems or ignore them, and it acts tirelessly. An example is Mother Theresa.

The second stage is called perkiness, and is represented by the snow lion, which plays in the highland meadows. It is able to engage with situations with joy and resourcefulness. A good leader has a vision and engages people along the way. He/she can relate to the emotional ups and downs of situations with resilience and humour. The example given was Martin Luther King.

The third stage is called outrageousness and is represented by the mythical bird *garuda*, which soars into the sky without any need to measure its accomplishments or compare itself with others. The leader is not afraid to question the status quo and initiate change, but still doesn't lose touch with the situation at hand. The example given for this stage was Mahatma Ghandi.

The fourth stage is called inscrutable, and is represented by a dragon. The dragon soars into heaven and then down into the earth, so it joins the two with perfect timing as the seasons unfold. The leader with this quality has the wisdom and skill to know what action is appropriate in which situation and allows the natural cycles of events (life and death) to take their course. The example given for this stage was Nelson Mandela.

The writer finishes with a quote from a business leader: "The success of an intervention is determined by the internal condition of the intervener". So it is this internal condition that a leader must cultivate if he/she wishes to be a good leader. Skills and knowledge are important, but they are not the core.

I found all this extremely helpful and illuminating. This is ancient wisdom, not a shallow idea that a management thinker dreamed up yesterday with a view to marketing. This is not to say we should soak it up unquestioningly. We should approach it with the inquirer's mind, trying it out to see how it fits.

*   *   *   *   *

A dream. There is a project, in the middle of the city, to unearth a structure that is buried. There is great curiosity and excitement about the structure. First I am an onlooker, and then a participant, shovelling earth to one side in order to clear the space.

The structure is an ornate colonnade, all carved and solid. It is uncertain what it is made of, perhaps stone, perhaps bronze. After the excavating it all lies bare, the earth scraped off it. It is not clear if it had been intended to serve a purpose, or what that purpose might be, but people are going to look at it for some time and ponder.

I think the dream was an allegory. It was about digging down below the level of consciousness and finding structures that are elaborate and magnificent but also mysterious. In the dream, the people uncover these things but they do not understand what they are, what they do or how they work.

I imagine that as people spend more time examining these structures, they learn something about them. I imagine that there are clues and discoveries and realisations, and a level of under-standing about what the structures are for precipitates. This is in the dream.

When I think about the people in the dream, I remember that they had different motives and reactions. For some, the whole excavation was just for entertainment and they enjoyed the feeling of wonder when the great structure was unearthed, but they were not so much interested in the speculation about its purposes. For others it was a serious business and the real work began after the structure was laid bare. They wanted to know what it was for. While others were sitting back and luxuriating in the moment, they were already down in the trenches with their hands dirty, feeling, tapping, examining.

When it comes to leaders, I think that generally this business of self-examination is treated dismissively. Leaders are about action. They like to make decisions, they have to keep moving, they have to impress their followers. Even when they are proven to be wrong and they have to reverse the direction, they still keep moving and urging people to follow. It's all about momentum.

It's easy to take decisiveness as the sole criterion of strong leadership, when it is actually useless and destructive unless it is partnered with astute awareness that is unencumbered by ego. So when we make assessments about the quality of leaders, we have to scrape off the earth and see what lies below. But the thing that bothers me about the dream is the nature of the materials the structure is made of. Stone? Bronze? I don't think so.

I think what makes the structures of our mind difficult to determine is that they are not solid like stone; they are dynamic and fluid. And the key to it is the part our ego plays. And further, the ego is only tameable when we cultivate unconditional confidence, when we cultivate the constant awareness that we are okay, in essence. Then we may begin to be a good leader, and only then.

I can see why the structure appeared to be made of something solid like bronze or stone, and was encrusted with earth after being buried. Our attitudes and habits become solidified and entrenched. They lose their inherent fluidity and dynamism. So yes, the elements of the dream make sense.

*   *   *   *   *

What am I left with? The concept that dreams occur occasionally to suggest directions to us. I speak only tentatively of knowledge. When people talk of knowledge it sounds so certain, yet the more significant the matter is, the less it seems to me that we can say for certain that we have knowledge about it. Certainty seems to be more pertinent to the mundane. I wore a blue shirt yesterday. I went shopping at six pm. The door is open.

But to say "He caused an argument" or "She was abrupt in her manner" is different territory. Here we have moved (so quickly) beyond the certainty of material facts. We are interpreting, we are making judgements, we are applying values. This is not to say that we are forced to be agnostic. No, we simply have to understand what we are doing, and share our assumptions. We are seeking to make sense of what people do, and using the concepts we have developed through our experience.

This is starting to sound obtuse, and yet we need to understand what is going on when we talk with each other about anything more than the colour of the shirt we wore yesterday, or what time we went shopping. My stories about my exodus from the city and about what I am doing back in the city are built up of a host of interpretations about a host of experiences. To make it even more exquisite, my very experiences are shaped by the attitudes and perceptions I bring to situations.

I remember one job I had, where after several years our unit was assigned a new manager, who, to everyone's dismay, was appalling to work for. She was a serial bully. She would pick on one employee, generally the youngest and most inexperienced, for weeks at a time, micro-managing them and belittling their skills. This was ironic, as her own knowledge of the work and the skills required to do it well were almost non-existent. After a few weeks, having wreaked damage, she would move onto someone else. She always had one person in her sights.

I was older and less susceptible to being bullied, so I wasn't targeted in this way. But I was still subjected to the stupidity of her decisions and I would frequently express my disagreement (not that it made any difference). Then I had a change of heart. I decided that I needed to leave. That was the only reasonable course of action. However, it took me some months to engineer my retreat, and I didn't want to leave on bad terms with the company.

Hence, I changed my attitude towards the manager. I

stopped arguing. I went along with whatever decisions she made, no matter how foolish I thought they were. I saw that she was perfectly convinced that what she was doing was what the company wanted her to do, and the truth is, it probably was. The other day I was driving alongside a river, in the traffic, waiting for the lights to change, and I noticed the water. The tide was coming in and the water was moving inwards from the ocean, quite fast, a great tidal surging. Who would try and stand against that?

Just so, I let the tide take its course. I had a quiet few months. I smiled and relaxed amid the grim machinations of the petty tyrant. A couple of the younger members of the team left and found more congenial situations elsewhere. The manager started gnawing into one of the older workers, a dedicated soul who had been with the company for more than twenty years. It was disgusting. Still, I had established that it was pointless to protest, so I said nothing. I talked with the person and sympathised. I observed that leaving was one option.

Finally I organised alternative work and the last day came. I refused the compulsory interview with human resources. I sent them a reply to their invitation saying that I would agree to the interview when they could provide me with information on what actions they had taken in response to the last hundred or so exit interviews. Perhaps that was a little provocative, but there was no love lost between myself and HR and everyone knew that.

The underling who was to have conducted the interview sent me a hasty response that it would not be necessary for the interview to be held. Ah, the HR department was ever determined to claim the ground of authority, even when it was an empty claim. Were they really going to force me to participate in a meaningless interview on my last day in the job?

But there was a meeting to be held with my manager. I couldn't avoid that. I had determined to retain my resolve to be polite and implacable. I smiled. Then she remarked to me on how much "our relationship" had improved over the last few months. I was hugely surprised by this remark. I hadn't thought that this might be the effect of my decision months ago. Well, what could I do but agree with her? "Yes, indeed it had." I smiled again.

And then it was good to walk out of that door.

My point? In most situations we are not dealing with safety and certainty. We are dealing with other people, who can be unpredictable and dangerous. How this occurs is affected by the attitude we bring. If I had this time over in that job, I would probably approach it differently. Both my initial attitude of feisty opposition and my subsequent attitude of silent acquiescence had an effect. And both attitudes were less than the Tibetan stance of unconditional confidence, so that effect was not what I would want now.

I would want to be fearless enough to be open to the whole situation and ready to be engaged. What I did, in effect, was to withdraw. I would want to find how to enable the corruption to rot away and how the old values of the company, which were noble, could be allowed to reassert themselves.

Of course, at some point one makes a judgement about what is possible in any situation. And I did make the judgement that I did not have the ability to have any real effect in this company. The leaders were intent on their path, they were adamant that anyone who thought otherwise should be rooted out and banished.

I accept that other people would have different accounts (stories) about this company and the behaviour of the people within it. Are our stories equal? In one sense, yes they are. I try and persuade you with my story, and they would try and persuade you with their story. It's a contest about who is the most persuasive. But how would this dialogue go?

Well, the manager would dispute the facts. She would say, "I've never bullied anyone. I'm just doing what a manager needs to do. The staff need to perform to a higher standard. We operate in a very competitive environment. Managers have to be strong."

But my stomach is not in this repartee. If it's accepted that the competitive environment is tough, her management style is still not the way to get higher performance. It is still bullying, and it just shows that the managers and the company have not figured out how to operate effectively in this environment. I would refer to studies that show how higher performance is achieved through building trust and encouraging collaboration and participation in decision-making.

It comes down to resonance. I would offer a framework that locates the behaviour of such managers in this framework and distinguishes their behaviour from more constructive ways of managing. And it is this framework, this picture, that would be compelling, because it would resonate. The picture would also show the managers how it is possible to be different, although it would not tell them how they would need to change. That's another story.

People say they need evidence. They talk about evidence-based management, evidence-based coaching, evidence-based teaching, et cetera. It does sound scientific and rational, and authoritative. But, for example, studies have found that companies that have ethics programs in place perform better on the stock market than companies that don't. So why don't all companies have ethics programs? Are the companies that don't have ethics programs not evidence-based? And all the ones that do are evidence-based? I don't think so.

The same is true of training programs. Companies that have comprehensive learning and development programs perform better on the stock market, over long periods of time. But when there is a business downturn, companies cut their training budgets. Where is the evidence base for this action?

What is more like the truth is that companies that have strong ethics programs or training programs have a culture that wants to be ethical and wants to foster ongoing employee development. It is part of their vision of themselves and how they want to be seen in society. Yes, their financial performance is better than other companies (on average) but that is not why they do it (thankfully). Can you imagine a company that only had ethics programs because they were good for the bottom line? Suppose one year their results were down. Maybe this is evidence that ethics programs don't pay off and they should drop the programs.

It's the story that sustains you. The evidence comes afterwards, and it's not always regular or uniform. I like the Johnson & Johnson story about product tampering in the 1980s. Someone tampered with their best-selling product, Tylenol, and put cyanide in it. Everyone only became aware of this after about six people had died in a short space of time. So, when Johnson &

Johnson realised, they had the choice to bluff their way through and hope the tampering had ended, or do the responsible thing and take the product off the shelves, everywhere.

This is a good news story for business ethics, because they decided to recall all the Tylenol from the market until the situation was sorted out. (No, they never found the culprits, that's the sad part.) It's a good news story because Johnson & Johnson did the responsible thing and kept Tylenol off the market until they had created tamper-proof packaging. It's a good news story because the decision cost them millions, but public faith was then restored in them and the product, and the company went on to recover their losses and increase their profits.

What we forget or under-play, from this point in time, is the extent of the risk those managers took. Their decision could have meant the demise of a huge company that had existed for nearly one hundred years. Was their decision evidence-based? Quite simply, no. There were facts that they needed to know, so there was evidence in that sense, but did the facts determine their decision? No, they didn't help. The managers had to face that decision on their own. They had to make the decision, in the real sense of "make". No calculations could have made the decision for them.

I say, with tongue in cheek, the most important thing in business is to get your story straight. Slippery business people find plenty of scope for fudging in this statement. They think you can survive and conquer as long as you make up a story and all your accomplices stick to it. Nowadays we see regular exposes of slippery people who discover that someone didn't want to stick to the crooked story any longer. The thing is, the story actually has to be straight if people are going to get their story straight together.

Straight means true, and aligned with values you can be comfortable with in public.

This is the case with the stories of our everyday lives. But there is a big story too. That's a bit different. The big story is the story that makes sense of everything. The big story was what had fallen to pieces for me when I had grown up and was at the stage of having to enter into society as a member, a working member. I didn't believe the big story that was being presented to me. I had to go away and try to make a new story. It's not an easy thing to do.

People might say I have not done anything much. Here I am back in the city that I'd left. That looks kind of circular. And I'm not asserting that the return is about a spiritual revelation, as in T.S. Eliot's verse (from *Four Quartets*):

> We shall not cease from exploration
> And the end of all our exploring
> Will be to arrive where we started
> And know the place for the first time.

No, it is about having a voice. When I left, I didn't know what to say about the city, I just knew I didn't feel nourished by it, I didn't feel it was nourishing for people generally. I spent a long time away in the country, and I could have stayed there. I lived next to a creek, and the water flowed past my house every day, fresh, clean and cold, out of the mountain.

The story is about finding an image that makes sense of living. This is the image I found. Whether we live in the city or the country, there is a source of life. It is the same for all of us. That's what water represents, the spirit that we all need to keep on living. We are of nature and we rely on sun and air and water and loving kindness. When we separate ourselves from this knowing, we become like muddy creeks. We have to keep close to the source, no matter where we live. It is harder to maintain this connection in the city, but it also cannot be assumed that people in the country have kept their connection with the source either.

So it is not as if I have decided that the city is okay after all. The source, the spirit, is available anywhere, as pure and endless as the water that comes out of the mountain. When you know that, you can live anywhere you need to be. Do I know this? Haven't I cast doubt upon knowledge?

I will modify what I said. I think about knowledge this way: the best foundation for knowledge is the foundation that makes the best sense of everything. Or, another way, our foundation makes more sense of more of our experience than any other explanation. So, for example, a man says he has to act a certain way at work, by which he means he feels he has to be dishonest and cruel, but he would never behave this way at home. This is not sustainable. It will tear your life apart in the end and kill you.

A solid foundation has to have one source. You have to figure out how to integrate all aspects of your life. But the man says it's too hard to change the workplace, and he has to support his family. That's how big the problem is. I still say to the man, "This is not sustainable. It will tear your life apart in the end and kill you."

I know.

It's just that trying to explain what I know takes words, many words, and they seldom seem to be good enough or clear enough. I wrote books. They presented ideas, frameworks, models, concepts. I thought all of this was useful. I still think so. The books didn't say everything, and they didn't even say all the important things, but they offered a way of looking at who we are, individually and collectively in this world.

But they blew away like dandelion seeds in the wind, the circle breaking up and dispersing into fragments unremembered. What came next was a story. If a conceptual framework did not take root, then perhaps a story would find purchase. It was a story that tore me open and I had to climb into the clouds to get it and bring it back down. It was one of those experiences when you are the rope, and heaven and hell are playing tug-of-war with you.

This is when you know that you know, or at least, you know that the fire runs through you. I burned like a log that will last for hours and you know that the heat will be utterly beautiful.

I do not know what comes after that. After a fire there is the cooling of the embers.

Perhaps there is just murmuring. Voices continue to carry on inside my head, but they are half-heard, at a distance. I do not know what conversation the voices are having. They are seldom angry or scared or happy, they seem to be just talking of ordinary things.

Someone else comes along with a book that is new. It is probably about leadership. It is probably accompanied by marketing and reviews that say it is new and important. Is it more important than the fifty or one hundred books on leadership that

I have read? Does it make them obsolete? Does it offer a great, significant insight and perspective?

Perhaps it does. I just can't say. I would have to carry out one hundred comparisons before I could draw that conclusion. The central question is, is it just that the new book is new? What if I could hold in my head, all at the one time, all the great insights and mental models of all the books I have read on leadership? What would be the result? Would everything fall magically into place like a jigsaw, and make sense? Or would it merely be pandemonium?

There are two things in life: ideas and practice. The ideas reside in mental models and truisms (rules for oneself), and in a satisfactory life they are the product of experience (practice). I can't possibly digest all that is being said and written about leadership (or anything else). I am reading less and I am reading faster, and I am spending less time thinking about what I read. I think, "Oh yes, this sounds like Covey or Kotter or Mintzberg or Peters" (or somebody else). Or, "Yes, interesting, but what do I do with it?" and it quickly fades away.

It is the idea of practice that grounds me. Ideas can be helpful or not helpful. More or less. Yes, I would want to repeat that: ideas can be helpful or not helpful. And point out that that this is different to saying something is true, because that is what people are asserting when they say their ideas are evidence-based. They want you to believe that what they are saying is compelling because it is true.

Very little about humans is true, because the moment you tell them it is true they set out to defy you. You tell a man he is a coward and he is affected by this, and then you observe that he changes his attitude and acts with bravery. So your evidence, past behaviour, is no longer relevant. Do you get the feeling that evidence is being wielded like a superstition? I think Kurt Vonnegut had a word for it, that he invented: "granfalloon". Beware of magical words like "evidence", because they are probably granfalloons.

So there is practice. Whatever the ideas in your head, and they do indeed have an effect on you, for better and for worse, there is always practice. There is what you do from day to day. It can be conscious or unconscious. And there is a constellation of

66

words that are associated with practice – stance, attitude, repetition, habit, laziness, discipline, devotion, faith, determination. Yes, this is personal. I cannot argue about these things. I have to stand in the light and see myself for what I am.

Part 2: The renewing

This is the burning water. This is the crossing of the river of life and death. This is the soul entering the great stream with vigour, retaining the centre and containing fear. Birds fly upwards. It is the season when fruits ripen.

I am a shape shifter at home in the dream world. I am on a campaign in the demon country, to find the roots of the world tree and dance at the spring festival. It is all good.

*   *   *   *   *

I begin the renewing with this incantation. This is the quest: to be satisfied to be here now. It's not enough to be told that that's all there is. Some would say, despite our lofty thoughts, most of our time is spent in the mundane. Looking at the clouded night sky hoping to see stars, just because. And looking at the food in the refrigerator trying to decide what to cook for dinner.

I chastise myself for getting to the end of the day not having done all the things I wanted to do, not even finished all the chores I should have done. Feeling better just because I did sweep the floor. Feeling worse because I haven't yet painted the bathroom. Feeling worse because there are probably many more things I could be doing, should be doing.

A journey through a day is like fireworks – first an explosion of brightness and beauty that looks like promise, then the slow dispersion as the points of light scatter from the centre and fade, extinguishing themselves, withdrawing into dark.

The morning comes again and I will gather into another explosion, and this time it will seem like perseverance, but then will come the grinding, the effort leaning against time to make small gains, so small against the daily losses. So hard to rest, and yet sleep beckons inexorably, even as dreams bring only bewilderment.

I know this is a matter of perspective, a way of looking, a way of seeing. What is to be said?

I have learned to stop. I have practised it. Others might say I have become less active. They might even say I have given up on goals. Where is my action to manifest a new career, let's say, as a writer? But I am in conversation with the ancients. The ancients don't say I should push on with the goals. They say I am a beginner, and I have much to learn. Their advice is to stop and retreat.

I wrote these lines as a guide for myself, a reminder of who I am and how to be:

> I breathe in, I breathe out.
> I set the omens at the four corners of the hidden lands –
> I set the omen of light before me,
> I set the omen of darkness behind me,
> I set the omen of thoughts and thinking to my left,
> and the omen of feelings and emotion to my right.
> I sit within the omens, where all light arises,
> breathing in, and out.
> I sit in the golden light,
> and blue light surrounds me.
> I am protected.
> I am grace, I am energy, I am love.
> I make a new day.
> Wordless, I let go of the striving.
> What is eternal is what is here
> in stillness.
> There is no separation from the infinite.
> I am older than the earth
> and days will take their place.

If I am entering into this experience, I must begin by accepting this space. There are no chapters, no headings, no structure. I just start here and go. What drives me is the need to reconcile this seesaw movement between centredness and dissipation. It is the desire to understand the nature of heaven and earth.

I recognise the amusement that the mention of "heaven" might cause. I learned about heaven in Sunday School, and it was written about in the Bible. I recognise that it evokes images of a cloud in the afterlife, where angels strum harps and the light is always gentle. But I am appropriating the word to signify the golden heart of all-that-is. I hope this makes it clear.

Yes, I am toying with you. What I am saying is that we are creatures of metaphor. The important things we want to express are only expressible that way. Heaven is the idea that we are more than physical matter; we are of spirit. It is not about a future state; it is not about an imagined alternative "non-physical" place. It is about an aspect of us now, all of us on this planet and in this universe.

Albert Einstein said there is no difference, it is all physical, because all that is physical is a form of energy, and all the energy in the universe is one.

The truth that we want to express is only accessible poetically. It is not the province of prose.

So, here begins a new journey. It is not a story yet. At the beginning of this journey there are many stories that have been told. There was the story of leaving the city and coming back. There was the story of going into the country and the story of coming back into society. There were stories about experiences with leadership in organisations. There were stories of relationships and family.

This journey could not begin before those stories had been told. But those stories are over. In the telling they became complete. The only point of a story is to enable you to make sense of an experience, encapsulate what you have learned from it, and live with more awareness and integrity. Of course, you might go back to an experience many times and find many stories within it. This is called deep understanding.

At the beginning of this journey I am grateful for having experienced much and for having learned lessons from all of this, but I am also wary of reducing all experiences to lessons. I learned this distinction by surprise. After the Woodstock music festival in 1969, Joni Mitchell wrote the song "Woodstock" to commemorate the event. She sang it, and Crosby, Stills, Nash & Young also did a version. Maybe I misheard this, but in one version I heard the line "Life is for living", while in the other version I heard "Life is

70

for learning".

That went over and over in my mind. If you say life is for living, do you overlook the learning? And if you say life is for learning, do you overlook the living? This is worth pondering. It comes down to what your stance is in everyday life. Are you open to it or are you just looking for the lesson? Or, are you just living in an unthinking way, unaware and unreflective?

In pondering this conundrum I was eager to get to an answer, to possess the answer, a definitive statement that wrapped it up ingeniously and astutely. Now I would say that the most important thing is that my answer is not glib. There is merit in both perspectives, and my goal ought to be to learn how to incorporate both perspectives in how I live. It is dynamic, and it is about performance.

I think of it like singers think about their performance, each night they go on stage. They know when they have done justice to a song, they know when they didn't get it right, and they know those nights when they transcended themselves and discovered a new personal horizon. This is how to approach living and learning. It's a performance art. Like the singer, the accomplished artist in living is able to just live, and yet somehow also be aware of it and process it for learning.

*   *   *   *   *

Does this mean there are no more stories? The new journey sounds like a repetition of practice, a cycle of affirming the good, attempting to remain true, failing or falling away, and then returning to start again. But it is not this way. The practice is your personal response to what comes your way, the constancy and the openness. The stories come because the world is different each time, it is changing and evolves from what happened before. New stories build on earlier ones, which are stories of how much or how little we all responded in the light of the Way.

The flow is subject to the factors, and subject most of all to us. Walk until your feet find rhythm. Sit quiet until you have sensed the presence of everything and everyone, desire, pain, sadness and confusion, love, vastness.

We all know the saying of Lao Tzu, "The journey of a thousand miles begins with one step". I say this is true, and I mean that I have experienced the truth of that statement. But there is another saying: "The last step is half the journey". This is a thought that extends me. I think, what is the experience it is suggesting?

It is to say that we are not complete, we are journeying. It is what has not happened yet that will complete us. My identity lies in the future, in the things I have not yet done. I think about what this means. It means that the future is the most important thing, because it will, in the end, define who I am. It makes sense. The woman who has been the competent secretary of an organisation for many years, and then decides, for whatever reasons going on in her head, to embezzle the organisation's funds, is defined finally by that embezzlement.

Likewise, consider the woman who has been an ordinary nurse, just interested in doing her job well, but who then encounters a doctor who is incompetent and who is causing injury, pain and death to multiple patients. She becomes determined to expose the doctor, and pursues her cause passionately and determinedly, until he is banned from practice. We define her, in the end, by her act of heroism.

It need not be an outstanding or atypical event that defines a person. It can be their constancy to the end in being loving, caring or impassioned, whatever quality it is, and maintaining that quality through all circumstances. One thinks of the humble, brave dedication of Aung Sun Suu Kyi in Burma (Mayanmar) over most of her lifetime.

This, after all, is the story. There are stories and stories, myriads of them, millions and billions of them. But we ache for something more. We ache for the story that has the ending that makes sense of everything, the ten thousand things. I heard another saying about stories: The story makes sense; if it doesn't make sense, the story is not over yet.

I know why there are stories. It is because if there was just practice, or duty, then our lives would merely be the serving out of a contract. They would not be interesting. But for better and for worse, our lives require our engagement, not the mere delivery

72

of dutiful service. Life comes to us untidy and in need of what we have, often sometimes when we don't even think we have it to give.

It takes all of us, down to the bottom, where Victor Frankl turns to us and says, "Who do you want to be? What meaning do you want your life to have?"

Moreover, we encourage each other. We give blessings to Aung Sun Suu Kyi and Nelson Mandela, that they decided to complete their lives by stepping into the vastness of loving kindness for others. That was the meaning they chose. We are encouraged by the way they chose to live their lives.

People like to judge. They say, "Well, Nelson Mandela achieved so much, and yet the situation is still less than satisfactory". But he wasn't the answer, he was just an example and a rallying point. Ultimately there is no answer until we are all the answer. And all he did was to live his life with the meaning he wanted it to have. He stepped into it and it became so.

He was not the master of the universe. Lao Tzu says, "The world is ruled by letting things take their course. It cannot be ruled by interfering." Lao Tzu spent less time explaining himself than most writers do. He is succinct but sometimes cryptic. Most of what I do in life could be called interfering. So I find this a difficult truth. Should I struggle with it? Occasionally I see that what he says holds truth. Aung Sun Suu Kyi was not interfering. I get it. You have to ask the question: interfering with what?

It was the Way of heaven and earth that she was not interfering with, the Tao. She was standing inside that meaning, she was following its course. So interfering is about what we do when we are not following the Way, and that happens when we are under the spell of our ego, which has two manifestations, the dominating one and the scared one.

Which leads to the question, can we live life fearlessly? This is clearly possible. People drive cars fast and jump out of aeroplanes with parachutes. Fearlessness is offered to us as a worthy attribute. But I question the pursuit of this single goal. What is happening with the ego?

Here is the revised version. Yes, it may be desirable to have a goal, and the goal may even be admirable, like fearlessness. But just as important is attending to the machinations of the ego, in both of its guises. For all the heroic rhetoric about goals and achievement, if we are not in tune with the Way, then we are just interfering with the universe. The fearlessness of driving over the crest of a hill on the wrong side of the road is therefore flawed. It is married to the ego that will go to extreme measures in order to either (a) have something to boast about (the dominator), or (b) belong to a group (the scared one).

*   *   *   *   *

What is the story now? It keeps changing. "Enough words have been exchanged. Now let me see some deeds." (I am informed that these words come from Goethe's work, *Faust*.)

Story hangs in the air. I have recounted stories that were meaningful to me, and I thought they might be meaningful to others. But it is so hard for people to listen, still harder for them to understand. You can tell others, but you also need to feel, at least sometimes, that someone understands your experience.

Sometimes I just write what I am experiencing. I don't know what I am doing. And I write without being read, much of the time. Aborigines ask, "If it's so important, why do you write it down? Why don't you talk it or sing it to the mob?" I talk on paper (or digitally, on computer). What can I say in response to them? I am a product of my culture. I am words that may never be read. Our mob has dissolved into larger aggregations, and within this, individuals fracture. The rest align with spectator sport and reality television.

There is no time for listening. Even songs are sampled, one second of this, two seconds of that, and compiled into a new offering. We are gratified because we get the value of six or more songs in just two minutes. It saves time. There is so much to listen to that we have to have earphones while we walk from place to place. There is no time for sitting and looking at landscape. Our thinking time is processed and packaged by others. The more accomplished among us digest all this with apparent grace and can proffer opinions on demand.

Much as I like the idea of technology – it promises power

and freedom – I resist the practice of it in my personal space. I cannot walk around with headphones on, I cannot imbibe ceaselessly. It is exhausting and, I suspect, fruitless. I worship the idea of the verandah, where you sit in late afternoon and observe the melting of day into dusk, the slow soaking of light into night. This is what our bodies want, indeed, crave. This is the central issue of our day, to unlearn the deafness we have to our bodies.

Do you know that when you softly seek to hear what is, moment to moment, tears well up? I guess that is why people resist the endeavour. I have given up the resistance. Curiously, living in this way I have discovered there are others who also wish to tread lightly and honour the earth and its people, and all creatures, all things. It is not a secret pact. There is no secret. What I do, I do in the open. It may be witnessed. I don't mind the sun on my face.

I know that some people are trying to reinvent local culture as the antidote to the emptiness of a technological life that is driven by a bottomless corporate lust for profit. But we have gone too far for that. We are networked into a global morass, and we have to reclaim our souls out of that morass. Our brothers and sisters are all around the planet, not just next door. I don't have to talk to all of you, I just have to know that you are there, and we all go back to the big bang, the one dot in space from which we all came.

I hear it when Aborigines chant, and they are chanting their humility in the big space of their land. I hear it with the singers I listen to, they are singing too in humility, they know that gentle hearts bring up children well. If you like, it is paradoxical that these gentle hearts are fierce when need be, when fierceness is needed to remain true to the Way.

I will tell you a story. It is about the nature of fierce hearts, and how they may be noticed. Picture: it is a music festival that goes for six days, an extraordinary thing in itself. It is a feast of different types of music. In six days, there is time for things to develop and take shape, and for things to happen.

So now it is New Year's Day, and it is hot. It is late morning, and the crowd is still thin, as many people are still sleeping from the night before. The music takes place in tents, big marquees with dirt floors and the sides up to let the air in. In this tent there is a band playing with practised design, creating sweet landscapes of sound.

This was a band that had been carving out its own space for over ten years. It knew its mastery of that space, swinging from grand to frolic, summoning trickle, flow and storm from guitar and fiddle, didgeridoo, piano, drums. Song was high and rhythm established.

A woman walks into the tent. She barely looks around. Barefoot, she enters the space and moves, picking up the time, tuning body to sound. People dance to give heed to music and the occasion of gathering with others. Or they dance to acknowledge the excitement of the music. Most often they dance in habitual moves, and with one eye on the censor, who is a shadow in the back row, ever-critical.

The censor says you must be careful not to look foolish, and the most cautious way to ensure this is to watch others and copy them. And when we are all in synchrony with that projected image, we have ground down our patterns to doggerel steps. We have a small repertoire of moves we all know, and we can look at each other and know we are safe.

The woman is not interested in safety. She does not dance to prove she is like others. Her feet and her body tell a story, and it is her own.

The band is above this. If they have a pact with dancers or with the audience, it is secret. They keep to their score, and the places it takes them. They soar, moan, laugh and affirm, they lilt, lament and beguile. They do it loud to shake the thin canvas of the tent, and they take moments into softness to suffuse the tent with gentle magic.

And the woman stomps her feet. Not heavy, but with firmness. Not clumsily; rather, with grace. Her feet are making a statement. What is it about? She stomps, and her feet meet the earth of the tent's floor. Stomp.

Around her there is the scattered flurry of other dancers. A young man on a backpacker's holiday from Europe, with wild, bright clothes purchased only this week. A young mother and her two-year-old daughter, sharing new adventures and whirling for fun. A woman in her forties taking her respite from corporate life and trying to remember what is worthwhile.

In among this, a tribal ceremony without precedent, a woman alone in a ritual of reconnection. Stomp on the earth, the earth that is our mother, the earth that gives birth to trees standing tall, the earth that bears our food and holds us as we sleep at night.

This is a dance of affirmation, of joy in feet meeting the solidity of earth, of gratefulness for each footfall and its answering thud. The strength is in her now, in her stomach, in her heart as she too whirls, carving an arc between other bodies and tracing the air with lightness.

Late-morning stragglers wander in and assume seats, enjoying the music's journey as they continue waking. The sun vies for attention as the heat rises.

In her soundless ritual, the dancer wears the heat with delicacy, perspiration at her throat and through her blouse. The meaning is in the movement as the band's story comes to completion. She arches her body with arms reaching out and up.

We know that trees live out of the earth's strength. We know that they sink their roots deep and wide, and build on that to climb through their trunk to the sky. We know that the branches of trees speak the glory of possibility, and the roar of leaves is deafening when the wind is wild.

There was no saying of this in words. There was the music, the longing of song, and the woman's feet beating out rhythm on earth. There was the quiet certainty in her performance. This was the renewal, allowing the strength of earth to enter her body, to find herself come again into grace and knowing what it feels like to be unafraid.

Then the going forth again. The woman picks up her bag from the chair and is quickly away. The band plays its last song, and there is sporadic clapping in a hot, late-morning tent at a music festival. People expend warm sentiments (fantastic, magnificent) and collect their bags.

That is the story. This is a fierce heart, at play, renewing itself.

*   *   *   *   *

Sometimes people have said to me: "You are a writer. You will write about this." I know they are asking me for understanding, not just to recount events but to interpret them. I have felt unworthy of their trust. I can summon glibness at times. At other times I can only trust and grasp after shadows, and hope that, like the painter, a brush stroke can tell a tale.

The rallying point for me has been ethics, with the necessary undertone of spirituality. At a writers' festival I heard a writer say "there is a moral shimmer around things". I wrote down the words to remember them.

There is a lot of explaining to do, but people tire easily. The answer has to be concise, and evident in the first sentence. But stories do not do that, they draw you into an experience that raises questions. The questions are usually about desires and threats. Some writers will say that the writer's work is not to give answers to these questions, but to ask the right questions.

I think there could be some doubt about this – some truth, but some doubt as well. It's just a little glib and dismissive. People get annoyed when you keep throwing questions at them and not at least infer some answers. I think most stories infer something, I mean, morally. If you end up feeling sympathy for a character who did something wrong and who hurt another person, you have at least accepted the landscape of morality. You accept that the question can be framed in a particular way, and that the character might have attempted a different solution to the problem.

Of course, that's the difference between discussing concepts and telling a story. With a discussion, you can always disagree with the proposition. But a story happened (even when it didn't; readers agree to suspend disbelief and accept the writer's fiction as real). You can't go back. It's a question of what we think about the things that happened.

But I don't think stories are sufficient. We also need to talk about stories and question the concepts they employ and imply. A powerful story might muster up sympathy for the devil, but then it would be good to delve into that feeling and ask ourselves why. The writer of stories will say that people go to stories, poetry and art to show them how to live, not to books on religion or philosophy. The writer will say that the central element of ethics is empathy. We act with regard for the well-being of others because we can empathise with how they feel.

I would include music as well. In music the heart is touched and pours out. Yes, but then we are back to propositions, and the need to qualify them. Not all music. Not the same music for all people – a particular piece of music may affect one person deeply but does not speak to another person the same way. Or it depends on the timing and the situation. Et cetera. Qualifications, disagreements.

I think the writers at the writers' festival were striving to occupy a simple position, that stories help people to feel empathy and the stories present the richness of life and don't offer a neat answer. I would want to differ in two ways. First, although writers do not generally set out their moral stance and assumptions explicitly, those things are implied by how they present their story and the characters. Even Camus and Sartre, in presenting characters who rejected (conventional) morality altogether, were adopting a particular stance towards morality.

Second, we need to understand our past. We tell stories about things that have happened because they raise questions about us and how we think we should live from now on. It is not just the recounting of things that have happened, no matter how intimately, forensically or sympathetically people and events are portrayed, that interests us. We want to know why it happened, and what it means to us now, and for how we will live from now on.

It is not enough to tell a story about how people suffered under a political regime, or how children suffered at the hands of priests. We want to know what it means morally, for us now. What would we do differently if it were us in that situation? As the victim? As a person in authority? As a witness? Going back a step, how would we avoid the situation developing?

There is also the question of the stance of the person telling the story. When I tell a story, it is the story that I am prepared to tell, and it comes from my perspective, along with any attitudes I have towards anything and anyone mentioned in the story. It incorporates my insights but it also reflects my blind spots. There is the danger of reading a story and taking it on as the single perspective on an episode. What would the story look like from another participant's perspective? What would that tell us that is different?

Considering these issues, what are stories to us? There is the enjoyment of them. That is one thing, and it could be the main thing, or the only thing. At the writers' festival I heard a writer say, "I was writing about that lovely silver light among the hills that you see from the river". She went on to say, "Mostly when I write I haven't got a clue what I'm doing. I just write what I'm experiencing."

Another writer said, "A poet and a writer of fiction have something to add to what the anthropologists (or any other scientists) say". We need to understand the earth and ourselves poetically. We are embodied, and our words need to reflect this experience. It makes a difference to how we live. It is not open to scientists to discuss ethics. Their mandate is simply to observe what happens, dispassionately, and to understand how it works.

Humans cross the boundary. We are not simply mechanisms that obey physical laws. What we feel, believe and value makes a difference to how we act. As it happens, stories make a difference too, otherwise we could make do with rules of conduct that we decided on pragmatically. That is, we could say, for example, society works better when people are forbidden from killing and hurting each other or stealing.

Albert Schweitzer said that there is nothing in nature that compels us to live ethically. Ethics are a choice that humans make. We cannot prove ethics from nature. We can say suggestive things about ethics, like, it seems that societies work better and people are happier when people behave ethically (as we choose to define that). We qualify it by saying "most of the time", or "in the long run", because we can all point to instances where unethical people seem to be prospering.

I like Schweitzer's approach. It gets rid of the desperate need to prove that ethics is like a law of nature. It is not. It is an arrangement that societies come to, and because most people agree to it, it is not surprising that we can discover evidence that when people and companies behave ethically, good outcomes occur more often than not.

But what the poets and the writers of fiction are alluding to is the idea that ethics comes from a deep well within us. Poetry, stories, music, art, they are the rope and the bucket that haul spirit from the depths of the well to exalt us. The job of the poet is to make us stop, and listen, and watch anew. To renew. And to renew, we must draw from what is beyond us, knowing that wisdom is out there, and available.

> This circus of thoughts
> that comes of reading –
> what one man thinks of concepts (versus reality),
> what one woman thinks of memory
> (a fateful geology or
> a fond but desperate grasp).
> It is all accelerating, it is
> a madman foaming at the mouth.
> The writings of men and women
> are a thousand beckoning mirrors,
> in soft light and harsh light,
> from above and below,
> and you know, eventually,
> you will have to drop the mirrors
> and hazard the broken glass
> and worse still,
> the absence of illusions.
>
> Look
> and there is the sage
> at your shoulder.
> Bewilderment and fate
> are now less compelling.
> You stop, turn,
> you read only to hear the voice
> of the sage
> who does not flatter you
> and who does not doubt you.
> You see there is a dance
> between fate and the sage

and you mark the steps of the sage,
to be able to be nimble yourself.
So you learn dancing –
from concepts to memories that are released,
from the comfort of memory
to the beckoning of a new future.
You are not afraid to step forth.

In new moments you know
that you must bring only your faithful self
that knows only the present
and who is prepared to swim
with the current
if the goal is everything
and if everything is love.

Which is to say, practice is one requirement for a good life, but inspiration is also required. Practice is about the discipline of regularity in whatever it is you do – yoga, tai chi, reading, meditation, chanting, singing, dance, art. But if practice suggests perfecting technique, then inspiration reminds us that you must bring your faithful self, it is your self that must be prepared to do what the moment requires in the world in which you partake.

There are two things in life: process and event. Practice is the process; acting in tune with the universe here and now is the event.

*　　*　　*　　*　　*

The distinguishing feature of stories, as opposed to exposition of concepts, is that they position you in a situation in real-time. You don't have the advantage of hindsight. When I write an exposition of concepts, I plan it, I set it out and make sure it is all self-consistent and relevant and adequate. In short, I apply many criteria to it and I might reshape it and restructure it many times before it is released. The finished product is coherent and logical.

With story, I am inside the process. I (or my characters) have to make decisions without full information, without a plan, just on the basis of what I or they bring to each moment. It is only subsequently that I can review what I did and consider whether my actions were wise or clever or kind. This is what I want the reader to experience through the vehicle of the story. Ethics as a performance art.

But there are those who think they have no need of stories. They feel they can make do with a manual or a set of rules. I would ask them to tell their story. They would say, "There is nothing to tell. I have a job, and I do it well, and I have gone from this position to that position and I contribute to the company and they reward me." It is routine.

In one sense this is fine, but there are flaws. First, I could ask, "What do other people think of you? Do they think you are a good boss?" Second, I could ask, "What if the situation changes? What would you think then?"

There is a fragility about the person who claims he/she has no need of story. There is a dependency on the universe to keep things the same, so that they can continue to follow the manual. Have you ever heard of a universe like this?

And there is a need to shut out alternative points of view. In this person's world, there is only one story. It is not even the dominant story; it is the only story. Many of us grew up this way. Many societies live this way. When you come across another society that has a different story, you kill them or conquer them. You give the survivors your story, and tell them it is the only one. This is why we need to talk about story.

The story I just talked about, the one you tell while you are in the midst of experiencing it, and before the end is known, is one kind of story. The other story I just talked about is the one you tell afterwards, which is the story you want people to get. It can be touched up and simplified, even sanitised. This is where there is room for versions of the truth, quite apart from the stories that are sheer lies or delusions.

This is like musicians doing different versions of a song; the sense and the feeling can be vastly different. I think of Led Zeppelin playing "Stairway to Heaven" – grand, magisterial, and then Rick Wakeman playing it on the piano like water bubbling in a hidden stream in the mountains.

So there is trouble with stories. People have made them up. No wonder the scientists are sceptical. They want us to say something definitive. But I won't give them what they can't have. The stories start where the science ends. What makes it really uncomfortable for the scientists is that they have to share this ground with us. They have to live here too.

I say, make an agreement. I say, summon the heart, and commit to act with regard for the well-being of others. Morality has no scientists, it has pastors and priests. It comes as an admonition and an exhortation.

"Ah, then", says the scientist, "morality is just about emotions".

You would think that a scientist would be more careful with distinctions. This is to say that everything that is not physics, chemistry or biology must be emotions. Life is more interesting than that. Beyond the material world that you can study as a scientist there is the world of us. To understand that you must talk about intellect (logical thinking and reasoning) and emotions (feelings), and you must also talk about moral values, and energy (or spirit) and the very act of awareness. This is a more comprehensive conversation, and a more satisfying one.

It occurs to me that you could talk about these dimensions without reference to stories. And I think of Tibetan Buddhism and its teaching of doctrine. They do not put story in the foreground. The emphasis is on teaching spiritual concepts and giving instructions for practices such as meditation.

But then there are the Aborigines, whose entire tradition seems to be rendered in stories. The rainbow serpent and the Dreamtime. And the Aboriginal saying: "The land is dying because no one is singing the songs" – the songs of the land. There is no word for belief. Nor is there any word for "thank you". Everyone in the community is part of a composite "thank".

I would understand the absence of a word for belief in the same way. It is not as if we stand over reality and choose whether or not to believe in it. We are part of it. It's more a question of whether it believes in us. So we must be worthy.

The Aboriginal stories and metaphors gather us in, they are not just about ancient past, they target our behaviour. We may

84

be like a crocodile or a crow, and that may mean greedy or cunning or some other quality (it will be clear). The community names its members and in this way moderates their behaviour collectively.

I have noted that the Tibetan Buddhists have stories too. But it's as if you must clean out your mind first. Listen to the instruction, learn to meditate regularly, slow your mind so that you are ready to hear deeper, more complex truths.

And us, our society? There are stories that traverse all of society, like the story about education. We all go to school when we are five, and do about twelve years of it. We learn certain kinds of things. It is only in the last thirty years or so that this has been true for almost all children. Both of my parents left school before they were fourteen. In another society, the big story may be about how girls go to school now, as well as boys. Or it might be about how only now most children are learning to read and write. Perhaps this is because previously there was a civil war raging.

There are stories that operate on a smaller scale, limited to a locality or a sport or a love of gardening. I am interested in stories about ethics in organisational life – whether people see ethics in terms of routine compliance with the prevailing organisational view, or whether they see the practice of ethics more problematically. If the latter, how do they characterise ethics? Is it about values they acquired growing up? Is it about how to reconcile regard for other people with corporate goals?

I can ask these questions, but I think I can only know what people mean when they tell me their stories of ethically significant moments. I want to know how such experiences moulded or transformed their perception of ethics. Did it mean they raised the bar for their personal behaviour? Did it mean that they made a more explicit commitment to adhere to ethical standards? Do they see ethical conduct as possible, or something you have to be prepared to compromise on?

Here is another quote from a writer at the writers' festival. She was talking about writing stories (fictional) that are situated in historical contexts. She said, "Stories are about interaction that breaks down existing perceptions and norms. The moment there is touch, things begin to change."

She meant the touch between the characters she had created and the accounts of the historical events. I know what she meant. In one story I wrote, the character, based on real life, resisted his own history and insisted on acting differently to what I had anticipated. In the end I bowed to him, I let him act as he wanted to in my story.

This is to say that I acknowledge the difficulty there may be in simply telling the story of any past event. We tend to read our current concepts and values backwards into the story we tell. Purists would struggle with this. They would want the story to be raw and unadorned. But my focus, if pushed, is on the developmental aspect of all this. Digging up the past has to be for some good purpose; it is not a mere hobby. I think that most people will see the difference between who they are now and who they were then, and might even be able to articulate what they feel they have learned. I approve of this.

> And secrets, secrets we do not have the courage
> to speak about, they remain undisclosed.
> All in good time, the rain falls. It wets everything.
> And when the sun comes again,
> on the corner there is a blind man
> playing the violin,
> and there is the peace
> each of us longs for.

I wonder about the person who wants to change their story. What if they speak it, or write it, and then they change their mind? They want to say more, or less, or present a different aspect that makes the story more acceptable or accurate for them? Having dug up the story and told it, they will remember more about it. It will come to them in dreams, some incident they had forgotten all about for years. They will want to add the incident, because they want me to understand what it was like, how painful, how difficult.

Yes, of course, I will accommodate them. I want to know. What it makes me more aware of is what telling the story means to the teller. It is validating. It says, "My experience was real, and significant". This is a moral issue, because the question we ask ourselves about significant events is, did I act with responsibility? Did I take control of myself and do the best I could?

So I have a function in this interaction apart from being a receiver of information. My function is to care, and in passing the story on in some way to others, to enable them to care as well. I learned this also at the writers' festival, from journalists who report on tumultuous and tragic events. Some journalists keep themselves distant; they take the story and run. In the business world you would describe this as being professional.

But, as it happens, these professionals often succumb in time to what the doctors call post-traumatic stress syndrome. In other words, it all catches up with them, all that grief and distress. The more human journalists deal with the situations more openly. They process things as they go. They talk to each other. They talk through what it means, and allow themselves to feel compassion, without wallowing. In accepting their vulnerability, they become more resilient. This is not hardness, but strength and wisdom.

Yet I am not the purveyor of judgements. I cannot say, you did the right thing, or the wrong thing. What if a person wants this from me? Do I evade the question?

There are two avenues. Either the person wants a comparison with other people, or a criterion they can use to evaluate their behaviour themselves. The "other people" measure is something like "You did better than most other people who have been in that position". The ethics criteria could include the classic questions: "Is it legal?", "Is it truthful, fair, harmful etc?", "Would you want to see it on the front page of the newspaper?"

I would feel comfortable offering a person a framework they could use to make their own judgements about their behaviour. They have to be responsible for their own conclusions. My role embraces understanding and sympathy, no more.

I observe that talking about story brings me to a realisation that roles are important in ethics too. What I should do in a situation is influenced by my role in the situation. If I were a teacher and two pupils were arguing I might intervene, but if I were simply a person walking past them down the street, I would not feel so obligated or entitled.

I maintain one rule with regard to roles: Before I am any

kind of role (teacher, manager, father, husband etc), I am a human being. Accordingly, if I were to walk past two school pupils arguing in the street, I still need to ask, as a fellow human being, is there a need for me to intervene to prevent a fight where one of them may be hurt? The human factor precedes all particular roles.

Similarly, in hearing a traumatic story, I need to ask myself if there is something I should do as a fellow human being, having regard to all the circumstances and using this definition of ethics: "having regard for the well-being of others".

*   *   *   *   *

These are localised stories, not the big story that explains everything. Am I happy with where I am now? Is there enough of a big story to go on with? I keep coming back to this, and each time there is a new aspect to explore. I need a good metaphor.

Many years ago I worked for a council, and the building inspector was talking to me about how the local soil affected houses. It expanded quite a lot when it got very wet and it shrank a lot when it got very dry. This meant that houses cracked – the walls, the ceilings, even the floors. Old wooden houses had some flexibility, but they could develop cracks too. Modern houses built on concrete pads could crack, but he said the idea was to construct the concrete pad in one piece, so that the whole house was like a raft that floated on the soil. That's one kind of foundation.

My old house was built on wooden stumps which were all independent of each other. But the house didn't move around much because the soil was very sandy and it was quite stable. So that's another kind of foundation.

When I think of big stories, I wonder if there is one big story that includes everything, so it is like a raft on which all the small stories float. This idea is popular. There are books on "the theory of everything". Other people think that the truth is more like my old house. There are many different stories that between them hold the house up. What do I think?

I believe in oneness and connectedness, as Lao Tzu describes it:

The Tao begot one.
One begot two.
Two begot three.
And three begot the ten thousand things.
The ten thousand things carry yin and embrace yang.

But here we are, in the midst of ten thousand things, and it is not easy to see the one story. As Einstein said, we should explain things as simply as we can, but not more simply than they are. I am happy to be an interpreter, relating individual stories to a larger context. This is a step towards the big story, without presuming too much. I want to understand personal experiences in a larger frame than the person telling me the story might have countenanced.

I have adopted three broad levels for ethics. I call them (1) law, (2) relationships, and (3) identity. What I like about this framework is that it gives me a connection from the basic level (obey the law) right through to good citizenship and spirituality (as I conceive it, in a non-religious way). The path can be described as a movement from compliance to reasonableness to intuition and imagination. This perspective transforms ethics from being a yes/no proposition to a "how much?" concept.

The development is also from outer to inner. The outer measure is firstly the law, then it moves to people in groups (or "tribes"; relationships become important to us) and lastly to inner directedness (personal commitment).

This I can understand. I find it personally useful. The big story is something else. It seems like the stuff of argument and contention. I am not seeking to be the master of the universe. If there is a big story, it is that society is changing, and the boundaries with other societies are dissolving, so instead of bouncing off the walls of our own room, sometimes our ideas penetrate through the walls to other rooms before they come back to us. It is often surprising.

In the meantime the business world seems to get meaner and more sterile, while token gestures of humanity abound. It is a world full of promises, it is all upbeat. But many companies are only measuring how big their promise has to be to hook you in. They are not intending to honour any promises, express or implied. This is the context, this is where ordinary people have to try and remain human while they are earning their living.

Hunger. There is still hunger. Managers in companies still want to treat their people well, but….. The environment is so tough, sales are down, there is constant pressure to cut costs.

New story. A new story is needed. How does a manager or a company get out of their current story and create a new story? And will a new story work? The problem is, they want to know that now, before they will do anything. They want guarantees. They want goals and targets and measures of success.

But note, the Tao is not called "the Goal", it is called "the Way". It is how companies are doing things that needs overhauling, not their goals. I suspect that employees are not even expecting generosity; they are merely expecting decency. Take responsibility, don't lie to employees, don't expect them to do things you are not prepared to do yourself, don't be greedy and selfish. People sense these things, they know when that is happening.

I venture that the main driver of unethical behaviour is fear. What is the source of the fear? I venture again that the main source of fear is fear of not being a success. This is where the underlying stories in our society make themselves known. Success is a glittering thing. It consists of flash clothes and cars, big mansions on the waterfront and lots of money in the bank. It consists of power over others, the ability to make other people slave to increase your wealth.

How do you disengage from this image? This is the key: commit to the Way rather than the Goal. This means you have to be prepared to lose. This is what makes you powerful, being prepared to lose worldly success in order to stay true to the Way. When you have done this, there can be no fear, because nothing can hurt you. All that is important is safe; you are invulnerable.

In truth we are wanderers and we walk in unknown lands. We try to predict, we try to control, we try to make it all simple, but the dynamics of every day are complex, tides and waves, short waves and long waves, and the surprises that people generate when they rub up against each other.

90

We are wanderers
despite the effort to be anchored in plans.
We are chosen to be in moments
we are unprepared for
just so we can learn to appreciate
that too, and that.
The wanderer learns not to presume,
not to depend on solidity,
however solid it may seem.
We wander best
with simple rules:
To enjoy.
To act with correctness.
To be bold but polite.
To know stillness in movement.
It is grand.

The renewal is every day.

Part 3: Onward

I am back in the room: the library, the office, the study. It carries all three names. I have nothing left, although the shelves are lined with books. They extend up to the ceiling. I have said all I could. What now?

I had a dream. I was at home and I went to sleep. I heard that one of the astronauts who had gone to the moon had died, and that he had left a recording of music from the moon. I didn't know what that meant – had he experienced the music and got some musicians to recreate it?

I had a device like an iPod, with headphones, and a lead which I plugged into a plug in the wall which was like a telephone socket, to pick up the recording. I was listening to the music, which was like violin music in space, with a poise like in "2001, A Space Odyssey", when I started to feel a sensation similar to being electrocuted. The energy was coming from the headphones and the music.

I tore off the headphones. The feeling I was experiencing was like a PowerPoint transition, one scene pixellating into another, but as if my body, my person, was actually being pixellated from one realm of experience into another. I was aware that some people might call this dying.

I stumbled into the next room, and the shuddering feeling was increasing, although I was no longer connected to the headphones or the lead, as if I really were transitioning from this realm into another, but I had no picture as yet of the new realm.

I was shaking. People asked me what was wrong, and I said, "Just get me a cup of tea." Then I woke up, still with the sensation of shuddering, or of being deconstructed pixel by pixel.

It was 3.00am. I got up and made a cup of tea. I was not frightened, but I was deeply disturbed. I do not have memorable dreams very often, and this dream was not just vivid, but real. This was me.

I think pixellating may happen when you are at a dead-end, namely, you have all the logic to analyse your situation accurately but none of the insight or power to alter it. Dreaming it is a vicarious experience of death. It acts the same way, in that it makes the new possible.

I take out a book of notes and read. It says, change comes to us, and transformation is how we deal with it, transformation of our heart-mind. When we dissolve our fixed patterns of thought we are inspired to move into the present imaginatively. Consider if you still have energy bound up in the past, and release it. Obstacles occur, but they are just obstacles, they are just happening now. You do not have to read the spectres of the past into these events. Continue on.

And I read this:

Ask what is helpful,
What is steadfast and upright.
See what is enough
And know
That it is sublime and abundant.

The question for me now is how I go forward. I let go of judgements and open myself to welcome what comes my way. Renewing occurs when you don't try to grasp and hold onto things, or try to control things. Just be aware of what comes, whether it is good or evil. Renewal means auspicious success in establishing the new.

This is the difficult thing, to rethink success, to see how it is a mistaken concept. The success that is venerated is temporary and unstable, like fame or winning. What is it that endures? Cosmic principle. And what is this? It is the attraction towards completeness, where forces harmonise. We shed incomplete visions continually, exchanging them for what is more inclusive, more expressive, more encompassing.

The ability we need is the ability to weigh things up and make them balance. The point of practice is to make this ability manifest in your daily life. It is the nature of Tao to raise up what is low and empty what is full. Tao blesses the humble so that they radiate the brilliance of Tao. When the humble person is in a low position, he does not lose the principle of Tao.

It is possible to take on difficult things, and to handle difficult situations that come to you, by emptying what is full, and filling up what is empty. Perhaps you have to experience many things and make many mistakes before you can realise this. It may be, that on a clear night, you see that the stars are a great multitude and you are witnessing it and you can steer your own life.

The girl stands on the stage and tells this story, and she is breathless. She realises this, and realises, now, that she becomes breathless when she is talking about something that she feels passionate about. This is a site of creative transformation. Brightness and awareness stir everything up.

It's okay now. I am stepping out to encounter the creative spirit, knowing that I am nourished. I do not consider the reward first, I consider whether the work is good for humanity. I am watching the world go by, waxing and waning. I accept strange omens, like the echidna that visited my garden in the middle of the suburb, and looked at me with his ancient eyes. He waddled all around the shelves I had just finished building on the verandah, as if approving, then wandered on his way. The cat stared at him disbelievingly. It was unprecedented and inexplicable.

I must go back to the ancient books and query the words and images, to understand power and virtue. I read, "Strange encounters will couple you with your new destiny". I don't care that some would find this obscure or bizarre. I wrote, years ago:

> Each our own way we must go to the desert
> where the angels will minister to us.

There is no refuge in the crowd. At some point you will find yourself alone. It is the shock of inner enlightenment that enables you to set real directions in your life. We all carry images in our heads from our parents, from our schools, churches, television programs, authority figures, friends and friends' parents. They establish the framework of our lives and the scope of our destiny. Our call is to see these images for what they are – conditional, circumstantial, not absolute.

Brought to awareness, the images will let you see if they are grounded in ancient virtue or are corruptions and mirages. This is the strange unfamiliar land that we must enter, looking behind the façade to see the pathways back to the source. This is where we make a fresh start. Remedying is needed. We have to make a new beginning.

Fortunately, although it seems I am only at the beginning, even after so long, the inner truth is that the journey is already complete. I embrace paradox. I am gentle and standing still, but I will also act decisively. I will not dally with minor problems, I will get to the root of the matter, and do what must be done to eradicate corruption. I examine myself for faults. I renew my ideals. There is a principle to follow.

Trust in the images that flow from the heart and the spirit that makes them true. With correctness there is joy. And the song soars.

*   *   *   *   *

I find myself going back, back into periods of time I had thought I had forgotten permanently. This seems to be required. If we wish to be here now we have to salvage all moments and redeem them. This is sometimes difficult. There are things I have done that I wish I had not done, and I cannot undo them. What is the point of going back there? I resist self-pity, I do not beg for forgiveness. Let the crimes stand, the infractions and the shortcomings. I stand in their shadow.

Nevertheless. That is what I have to say about that. I note that there is music, there is rhythm, nevertheless. It is a sign that the universe has the capacity to forgive, to absorb wrongdoing in the vastness of its liveliness, which otherwise we may call love and grace. It seems that the reach of forgiveness is extraordinary. It is even frightening.

A fire burns. Life, after all, is elemental. I sit before sticks that burn, logs that growl and mutter and consume all that needs to be eradicated. The effect that I feel is warmth on a cold night. I am gratified. I go deeper into the small sounds the fire makes, the intermittent crackle, the log falling apart, the hum among absorbing colours.

For a time, the passing of time does not matter, it is just an aspect of the life that we know. For a time, there is no need to summon spirits. There is simply no need. Others might describe this differently, but I am not them. I have to say it this way. I wrote this, in an earlier time:

> We know what is different,
> enough to own when time is progress,
> but we are out here now alone,
> having to question what we possess.

These lines never leave me. I am forever alert to occasions when I may have to question what it is I possess. There is no doubt I am alone; that much has changed. Otherwise, the sentiment is the same. However, I understand now, there is no need to possess. And I even understand what it means to understand something. You feel it in your bones, or even deeper; it is not just an attractive concept.

So it is an interesting phenomenon, the passing of time, and the changes that may ensue, the knowing that comes into play. There is so much I don't feel the need to prove anymore. I enjoy. I know that "enjoy" is supposed to be a transitive verb, but isn't it interesting when you don't provide an object? I just enjoy. What? I just enjoy.

Which means I have shaken off noise and chatter, neediness and worse. That makes you like resonance in space. It makes you like a grand piano played in a beautiful hall. The notes are loud and rich and fill the hall. The audience is profoundly silent in wonder at the richness and lyricism of the notes that are being played. That is what enjoyment is like.

I read these words in a book of the ancients: "When you disentangle yourself from vanity, anger, lust, hatred and the desire for revenge, you will open up a whole new cycle of time". The book says "There is the wang demon who carries disease and disorder, and there are the wu intermediaries who drive out the demons. Centre yourself and the body will align with heaven and transform your awareness."

96

A new story begins to unfold. It is the time of the moon almost full. The man who is a wanderer has discovered that people he thought were kindred spirits are in fact on a different path. There is no connection, and he cuts off relations with them. The abruptness of his actions surprises onlookers, for he is alone now. They think all the thoughts that people might think about this situation. Yet what they see is a man who no longer mingles. He is a question rather than a model.

The man is Mu. He names himself after the world tree that is anchored to the centre of the earth and which sees everything on the face of the earth between sun and moon. He has wandered for many months, and each day he has chanted the names of the elementals for hours – wood and thunder, water, mist and lake, golden light, mountain, earth, ghost river. He has named the wang demon and the priestess of the spring festival. He sings these songs as if he were an Aborigine, singing the song of the land so that it remains known and so that all will be well.

Now he has stopped the chant. He has encountered death and pure sorrow, and it has marked an ending to his course. He does not know what comes next. He knows this is a time of disconnection and that he has to deal with it impersonally. Yet he knows he cannot deal with this at home. Men and women come together at the festival.

He finds words for the time, a singing of the mystery of joy and sorrow intertwined.

> The other half is happiness,
> time as full
> as the meaning of a tree
> which is a tree which is a tree
>
> words fall away
> to leave us inside and outside complete.
> There is ever so much
> ahead
> and struggles, lessons
>
> I let go the future

here I
dwell in all fullness

sadness and joy pass
I take it
we are here,
the horror, impossibility
of any hope
of any room to exist
in the simple integrity
of earth-flowing manhood

I am the ache
in the heart of all plunderers
but here too
I am
all love
a wedge driven into heaven,
drunk on wild pure certainties

the other half is happiness
I am here in happiness
I grin like a fault
in the smooth face of illusions

(gentle should be
the fall into truth)

Mu is off to the festival to be immersed, to walk among
ordinary people, veteran alternatives and ground-level musicians.
Significantly, the musicians include both old and young. This is
surprising to Mu, although it appears natural when he is there
among them. After months of chanting and silent roaming he has
emptied himself of all memory of continuity. His last memories
of people gathering go back many years.

Mu is clearing the channels. He walks around the festival,
sits and listens to music, listens to people talking, listens to speak-
ers extolling the merits of living in balance with the earth. It is

both new and familiar. It is as if the boundary men are laying out the markings of the farming plots and villages all over again, as if to say, start over. There is a harmonious way. It will nourish you.

Mu sits in the shade of a tree on the hillside, listening to a band in the marquee nearby. It is lazy summer, it is holidays and people are strolling around and laughing with friends, or just dozing, but the band is performing with heart. And they are songs of the heart. They must have written them while most other people were doing business.

When people are busy doing business they forget that this is not the only reality. They forget that no matter how challenging it gets and how necessary it seems, the fullness of life has other facets, that cannot be judged by the size or security of the salary. Sometimes people have to take time to do other things – stop, be numb, sing, paint or garden, create sculptures or visit family. It may take weeks or months. For some people it takes a lifetime.

Mu listens to the music and hears the elements, wind and home, heart and fire, rock and sorrow and love. He thinks what it might mean. It unfolds this way…..

In the beginning there is just being. But after a while, being involves action. There is giving and taking – getting what we need and responding to the needs of others. Things move beyond the beginning. We enter the homeland of the physical – our body and its habitat. In the habitat there are harsh winters and lush harvests. We make our way. We feast in the times of plenty, but we must always be as alert as cats in unknown territory.

It is here that the lessons assail us. We hold tightly what we need and then we discover another who needs some of what we hold. Or we walk empty-handed in search of what we need, and find another whose hands are loaded.

What is the lesson? It seems that a lesson is in the offering if we stay alert.

This is not all. After the needs, there is sitting at campfires after a full meal and asking, what is more? After the needs there is reaching for purpose, and more lessons.

This is a mystery. Mu rejects the questers who venture to far lands and come back with a packaged truth: "the purpose is being". No, that is not what the chanting was for. The chanting was to summon all the elements that are here and call them to take shape, to frolic and cavort until they and we have made something new. We would be creators – of cities, electricity, knowledge economies, space stations. We would be artists and entertainers. We would be grand. Being was only the beginning. We would soar.

The music is for reminding ourselves that all the drive and the doing are for nought if we are not grounded. Achievement is not about winning, it is about expressing what is in the heart, giving voice to what the heart needs. Mu's job is to see what is important. He sees it one day in the tent where chai is served. There are two performers to begin with, who are Japanese, dressed in traditional costume, playing a formal, traditional Japanese air with a two-stringed lute. It is lovely.

But then, as they keep playing, onto the stage come a trio, a Celtic assortment with a fiddle, a flute and a guitar. Mu thinks, no, this can't work. These are two totally different cultures, from opposite sides of the world. But the two worlds proceed to blend. It is delightful, and Mu begins to think that strange worlds can intersect with harmony.

And it is not over yet. Along the back of the stage comes a young Aboriginal man, playing a didgeridoo. And again Mu thinks, this is going too far, this is not possible. And again they prove him wrong. They play wonderful music together, the Japanese, the Celtic and the Aboriginal. It is weaving separate worlds together and making something new and beautiful. Mu is silent but the cup is full.

*　　*　　*　　*　　*

It rains. From the hot sky come dark rolling clouds and the temperature falls. The rain starts lightly, drop by drop, and people look this way and that, like startled animals, looking for places of shelter. The rain increases tempo out of its darkened sky, taking over. Mu thinks of the words, "The rain wets everything". It is so complete.

The dust turns to mud and sticks to his feet. The water has no time to melt into the earth, it runs along the surface, coming from everywhere, the four directions. Two children are running in it, stamping their feet in suddenly formed puddles and splashing the water up. Mu sees people walking doggedly along the roadway, their shoulders hunched against the onslaught, faces bent down to avoid the battering of the rain drops.

Mu finds sufficient shelter under the flap of a tent. The music gives way for a time. The rain is too loud. Attention shifts from the stage to the wetting of everything. It is like a ceremony. Mu hears a contrary voice. It says, "Don't make too much of this. It is just rain. It is just weather, an instance in a statistical pattern, an expression of variables. And it's a risk factor for revenue, if people decide to go home."

He hears, "Always have a plan." But the voice sounds different here. With his head still filled with the sound of disparate cultures weaving together in a song, and thinking that this is new and momentous, the voice of prudence and practicality is, at least for now, muted. It is not wrong, it doesn't have to be wrong, it is just limited and less important. It is like a man with a tape measure when the sky is performing a symphony.

Mu says, "Can you hear? It is important to hear."

A voice answers. A woman smiles at him quizzically. "Yes, I would say so."

"Oh," says Mu. "I didn't realise I was talking aloud."

"If it's any consolation, you didn't sound crazy."

Mu smiles with a touch of embarrassment.

"What did you mean, it is important to hear?"

"I was listening to the rain, trying not to measure it and reduce it to a weather report."

She smiles again, "But we find ourselves having to be practical. It's hard to keep the child alive." They are both watching the children play.

"It takes hunger. Generally. When you have experienced drought, then you can learn to appreciate the experience of rain like children do."

"Generally. But that's not the point, is it? The point is to appreciate the rain anyway, without the need for drought." She is not arguing with him. She is carrying Mu's thought to the next place.

"And sunshine."

"And winter."

They are silent again. They stand adjacent, just under the edge of the tent, chatter all around them, amid the excitement of a storm, and the voices of people louder over the noise of the rain hitting everything.

"Would you drink tea with me?"

"Yes."

It seems that this has to happen in a serious way, where modesty and caution join the company too.

Tea means chai tea, at the festival. It means milling in a day-long throng of people who check in with friends, check out again and promise to meet later. It means conversations between friends who haven't met for many months or even years. It means gatherings of friends who see each other every day, so this is like another lounge room. It means a procession of musicians who may have never played in public before, or members of bands who just want play a little on the side, or test out something a bit different.

Facts. Mu is coming out of retreat with difficulty. Becoming familiar with someone means having to exchange facts, a tentative negotiation of what is interesting and what seems to be necessary. The song is still in his head and the rhythm, but there is also a desire to connect. The lady seems to be patient with him. She tells him history, people and circumstance, but she is selective, she is not going to burden him with every teardrop.

After all, they are here now, and that is a fact of great moment. It could have been otherwise. That sickness she had experienced could have been the end of it for her, that accident he had had could have been the end for him. For both of them these days the mornings break with wonder. They hear the first birds having anticipated them, and feel a deep sense of the rightness of things, perfection.

So it is an easy conversation. They are strangers but there is a plane where each of them could speak from inside the other. That familiarity is available to them. They tread carefully because of the wonder of this.

It still takes human effort to determine when they should part and when they will meet again. She has to do this, Mu has to do that, it is back to circumstances.

Mu climbs up to the top of a hill and stands looking out at the hills surrounding. There is light all around and above there are puffed bags of clouds, more for colour than for substance. He holds his hands out wide like Mu, the world tree. He feels his feet as roots going down to the centre of the earth. In this left hand there is the moon, and in his right hand the sun. It is a cycle of time wherein life breathes in, breathes out, grows to maturity and utters ripe fruit. There are no tears here. The understanding is immense.

Perhaps Mu is no longer breathing. He is standing still, arms like branches shedding blessings. The feeling is going down, down into the earth and up, up into the air, a glorious exchange and transmutation. After a time he returns to his body and moves, sitting down among a group of people who came to see the sunset. A girl asks, "What was happening then? I felt something was happening, but I don't know what it was. It moved me. Was it spirit?"

"Yes," says Mu, "it was spirit. But then, it is all spirit. Listen now."

And the wind has started up. Mu says, "The wind has started up so that we can see how big the trees are, and how strong is the connection between the earth and the sky."

The trees are certainly large. They must have many thousands of leaves, and each one communes with the wind, and talks with its neighbours about it. Each rustle is a small story, but each rustle is taken up and wafted off. The stories of the leaves are chasing the hills to tell them, to share what they have heard and put the sighing of human hearts to rest.

"Is this true?" asks the girl.

"Yes," says Mu. "Your stories have been heard. This is how you are able to live tomorrow. The wind is blowing away the sorrow that is stubborn, it is loosening you. There is more. Next you must listen for the sound of frogs in the twilight, and find sweet music to dance to. In the morning you will be able to forgive everyone who has ever wronged you."

Mu wanders back down into the temporary village. All is festive. How quickly the rain passed, and the ground dried. The lady is waiting in a food tent. They order meals. Everything tastes good. They eat slowly. Or perhaps they don't, perhaps it is just that time is moving slowly. The lady has been a mother a long time. Her children are all around her, even though her and Mu are sitting alone.

One of the children is sick. She is thinking, what could I be doing now to help him? But she has been there, she has made sure that he is mastering his passage through the illness. And she cannot do that for him. Yes, that is the part she is finding hardest. But, perhaps also, this is her safety, from the danger, the risk, of an unknown man. It is refuge.

Who is to say? Later, Mu's friends will say he manifested someone who was unavailable, because it suited his own sense of fear. Others will not register the episode at all. They will see Mu as the chanter, the lone cry of the elements, striving to call it into harmony.

Mu and the lady finish their meal and go to another music session. This time the artist is young, a girl with a guitar, singing. It could have been awful, and it was bound to be unschooled. Fortunately, the festival is the crèche for those who are ready to grow into greatness. It is the learning ground. So Mu and the lady listen attentively. In this place they know they are the elders and this is their vocation.

The girl finishes her last song and receives the appreciative applause. She has one last thing to say. She talks straight into the microphone and says, "Thank you for giving me your attention. I appreciate it. I am a musician. This is what I do, and it's great to have you listen."

And Mu wonders if this is the first time she has said, in public, "I am a musician". And he realises, once again, that it is important what you give your attention to. "Blessings," he says quietly. The lady gazes at him then, deeply. Heart moves.

The session is finished and people straggle in leaving. What Mu and the lady, or anyone else, have not noticed is that the sky has darkened again and when they emerge into the night the rain is beginning to fall again, a slack falling of masses of rain-drops this time, a heavy wall around them. They take shelter in the lee of a tree. Strange, that, the trunk of a tree in the middle of a temporary village, a trunk that was erstwhile in the unnoticed

104

open space of a valley.

They are hugging, unburdened from history, his or hers. They are kissing on the lips as if there were no impediments anymore. They are shedding and welcoming and consuming. There has not been time to differentiate these elements. They compound and coalesce. Their kissing is the squeeze of ancient beauty. Longing and its answer.

Ah, the demons are bound to return all too soon. Later will be time for tears, or whatever their substitute is.

The silence is long. That is how it was after the chanting, when Yunwin gathered up the scanty belongings that served them both, and used her wits to summon food and lodgings for them both. Mu remembers how he was nothing but a voice, and she sustained them both; her, a mere child.

"I was a leader, and a follower". Mu does not know how the young singers know these things, but they do. He can only be humble because he is unable to deny that he is a leader, but he does not know what the import is of what he does, and all he really does is follow. He tunes into the universe, he chants all-that-is for small people who would be free.

I can tell you what happened to Mu. The festival ended, and he went to see the lady at her home. On the way there he visited an exhibition of paintings by monks of old. And then he visited the lady, and had dinner with her and her children. And talked with her in the falling dusk as if there were no time. But there was, and circumstance.

Afterwards, he wrote this down. The poem defers to the monks who had attained implacability:

> The sun rises over jigsaw of buildings,
> this is a season benign but delicate,
> breezes lilting across morning shadows,
> with young women neatly attired and intent
> on making the office in time.
> Around a corner a throng of early risers chatters,
> bound for leisure pursuits
> in a jauntily painted bus.

Breathe in, breathe out,
sip tea,
stretch for openness, vast goals,
or none whatsoever.
Recall the dreaming monks
in mountains who,
day in, day out,
committed the silence to memory
and painted the cherry blossoms
for eternity.
Breathe in the chatter, the eagerness, the expecting,
and out.

Quell the tempests
and carry the smile.
Today the monk is travelling
to a crowded village.
He will be watching in the town square,
observing the crows cawing
on scrappy fences,
and the farmer straining
to haul the obstinate ox across the bridge.
He will repaint the canvas.

Because what we know is that the possibility was thwarted,
and both the lady and Mu bowed to circumstance. Perhaps for
others the time is not over, but for them it was. The monk realises
this and that is why he repaints the canvas. He is exercising compassion. When he is finished he averts his eyes.

Mu climbs up the hill again, on another morning. The sun
has not altered its stance. Nearby on the hilltop, a crazy-haired
youth is in the grip of a presentiment: the mothership is coming.
Mu sighs. "I understand". He does not realise he is talking out
loud.

"How could you know?" cries the youth. "What would you
know?"

Mu answers, "The mothership has been delayed. You are
here for another day."

And assuredly, the mothership does not arrive. It appears as if Mu is correct. But Mu is impatient. "I have nothing to say to you," he says to the youth. "Go away."

What happened to the teacher teaching tirelessly?

It is not grief. Or even impatience. Sometimes tolerance is merely indulgence. He has heard it in music: a sudden halt that is in rhythm but is an encapsulation of change. The greater work contains a disjunction, to end something that is rotting. In the music, as if to confirm this, in the background there is the sound of bagpipes, the hum of singers who know a better tune is possible. It will break out soon if the old tune is extinguished.

The lady is not there. She could have been, but she is gone, already. Too soon. He remembers he has held her. He casts ropes into the vast morning sky, knowing they will harness no stars or moons. He stands in a different kind of stillness. This time it has the quality of pensive piano, the keyboard rendering the way he is forbearing. The less sympathetic might think this is the universe mocking, but not Mu. He stands in the centre, and I have never seen him stand so tall.

All will be gathered. He goes back down the hill.

"I have a story," he says on stage. It is in the wake of the veteran performer that he has just listened to. Mu has listened to him for an hour, carried along. He remembers an experience where he saw a live band, and they were clinically correct. They gave a flawless performance, just like their record he had heard. He had been impressed, but directly after the performance they had put on a recording of the band: the same band, the same songs.

And it was disturbing. What was it he had heard just before? Was it the real band? Or just a recording of them, which they had mimed convincingly? He had felt cheated.

That was not the feeling here. This had been live. In fact, it was stronger than that. It was as if the singer had had something he wanted to get out, to express, and he didn't leave the stage until he had expressed every last ounce of it. And it was this night's feeling, everything – the festival, the storm, the melting of people into one, even Mu on the hill, and the leaves with their secrets.

Mu had felt it.

"I have a story," he says. "But it is no more than that. And on another night it would be a different story. Nevertheless, I tell you a story."

"Yes, yes," say the crowd. "We would hear you."

So Mu tells a story.

I knew a man, a young man whose name was Stone and who honoured the terms of stone, which is hard and difficult to gather and to work. He fled from the city, as many of us did, and cried in the wilderness for a season. But eventually he had to honour his word, and begin to work in stone. He was ordinary, a product of an ordinary family in a moribund suburb of the city. When you are born so, you grow up to think that everything above you is beyond you.

But he broke out of the city. It is no matter that he spent the first few months wild, smoking and pitying himself and raging. There were parties and fights and pounding music. After a time he assumed a stance, which was cynicism. You might see this as deficient, but cynicism is a man with ideals who does not wish to be violent. There is honour in this. And he began to work in stone. He took it seriously. He laid a concrete pad that would take him years to populate with stone to make walls to make a house.

The music played. All kinds of music. The music was to make time pass, and to lift his spirit from the moribund suburb from which he had extricated himself, though perhaps not all of himself yet. Yet he was trying. Every stone that he found was helping to form a new thing, his house. The stones would fit together and make a new whole. He just had to figure out how they fitted together.

There was a lady. She fitted in. The partnership between them was natural. There was a house that they were building, the two of them. He gathered the stones, and she willed them together in spirit. The house depended on her as much as on him. Perhaps in her mind there were images of ancient homesteads from centuries ago and countries ago, where honest folk lived whole-heartedly.

So it went, for three years. The stones were continually, albeit slowly, gathered. On the verandahs of friends in summer there were smokes and drinks that were interludes, and the laughter that cynics allow themselves, a dry and coarse version of the

108

real thing. The lady was usually seen in his company, as a retiring female presence, which was taken for traditional, dutiful submission.

I would wish to play music here, to prepare you. It would be clanging, jangly guitar, enough to lull you into accepting the roll of possibility's dice. You would know that something was going to come into this space, and I would want you to know that however horrible it was, Jesus would extend his arms wide enough to include it all.

The lady went away for a weekend, back to her home ground. And there was a key change. The story shifted. Music tells it best, a sustain on the keyboard, a growl from the guitar. She rang to tell him that she was leaving. What? What about all.....? But the guitars play a grungy rhythm that indicates the change has substance.

The news is followed by another revelation, a pregnancy. This puts a seal on the chasm between them. It is not just a leaving, there is a new boyfriend, who apparently has seized the long game. Of course there is irony. There wasn't meant to be a child. Instead there was rhetoric about the horror of future life on the planet. It turns out that cynicism is the shallow option. Parenthood is more primal.

So there is more smoking, and this time, much more of a licence to do so. Friends share in this, because that is what friends do. How does the story go? I report that there was a slow extrication from the decline. The concrete pad was still sitting there, and it was a worthy cause.

There were stones that beckoned to be sorted and placed one upon another, there was the ghost of a house that had not yet been built. If it had lived in her head, now it had to live in his. He heard, in the music that came his way, the melody of the completion. He returned, and the stones began to speak their language.

A long time passed, and I leave you with a mystery. The stone man appears at the festival, stripped to the waist, and in the company of a girl who must be barely out of high school. His hair has grown, it descends from his shoulders in an unlikely cascade down to the belt of his jeans. The girl wears barely a singlet and shorts and she fondles him, her breasts against him as if she discovered sex just yesterday.

In one way it is lovely and enlivening. One thinks of love and renewal and a new generation keeping the idea of love alive. But I am thinking about what the other lady thinks now, indeed, what she thought then. Who's happy, or was happy? No, it's not about you or me, it's about what could be, and whether that's possible at all, for any of us.

Mu ends his story and he is acknowledged warmly. But he comes off stage and an agitated man comes up to him, saying, "Really, is that your story? What are you trying to say?"

And Mu responds. He says, "No, actually, there is one more thing. The stone man knew me. We were neighbours. And I saw him here, with the young girl. And you know what? He acted as if he didn't know me. That's the real story. What do you make of that? What?"

Of course there is no answer. The man is stunned. He doesn't know what this could mean. But he does know that it is important, central.

Mu quotes from a song (it is Neil Young): "No one wins. It's a war of man."

He turns to depart. He has another quote: "You're the harmony to my heartbeat, baby".

The man responds, somewhat flatly, "So what do you say, after the flippancy?"

Mu laughs. "Life can end when you have salvaged all the moments of your life. Unless you give up, and then life can end any time. Or you get exhausted, like old people do."

Fortunately there is more music. Mu finds one more concert before he retires to sleep for the night. It is late, so late that birds are asleep, frogs are not croaking, cicadas have retired earlier. Mu laughs and stumbles towards bed.

He knows, he knows the question that morning will bring. What does it mean to salvage moments?

*   *   *   *   *

Mu wants more time, but it is morning. There is no fending off questions. But he says, "Yes, there is that question. But I will put it aside until I have ushered in the dawn. Properly. He says, "Consider the elements. Of which we are constituted."

And he recites the recitation for meditation:

I breathe in, I breathe out.
Breathe in, breathe out.
I set the omens at the four corners of the hidden lands –
I set the omen of light before me,
I set the omen of darkness behind me,
I set the omen of thoughts and thinking to my left,
and the omen of feelings and emotion to my right.
I sit within the omens, where all light arises,
breathing in, and out.
I sit in the golden light,
and blue light surrounds me,
I am protected.
I am grace, I am energy, I am love.
I make a new day.
Wordless, I let go of the striving
to be eternal.
Here,
merely being still,
I am infinite.
I am older than the earth
and days will take their place.

Mu says, "I close my eyes, and dream about changing. Now we may begin."

Before you die, you will go back over all moments, all the moments of your life. It does not matter if you were a wonderful success, in the terms that the world understands. The world only understands what it can see. You know the inside story, the one that you will be forgiven for or condemned for. Now it is a question of whether you will stand in the open and accept the judgement. There is no one present, just you and eternity.

Do that, for all moments. Accept the judgement. It is just. This is the moment when you are not running. Do you see that you are surrounded by love? Today you can have a feeling you have never had before.

There is a great ceremony on the last night of the festival. People gather around the hillside in the thousands. There is a choir of five hundred people, men and women singing in four-part harmony, parts they have learned just in the last few days. There is a grand-scale drama played out in the open space of the paddock, with giant effigies made of paper, colour and lights. It is a story, an allegory of humour and irony and hope.

At the end all the effigies are set alight and they blaze up to the sky, burning and then collapsing slowly, falling to the ground to become formless ash. It is like Aborigines departing from a camp site; nothing is left behind. What was enjoyed is inside of all of us. There is no need for monuments.

This last time when people walk down the hill, it is quiet. This night it is a congregation of quiet walking, the gathered sound of a multitude holding that moment inside, not to forget in the world they are returning to. It is love, it is hope, it is humility, it is humour and creation, it is individual but in some way it is all one.

When Mu returns to his tent, a long walk down and up and around the hillside and near to tall trees, there is a tawny frogmouth owl sitting on a low branch near the tent. The tawny frogmouth is the owner of the night, it speaks to spirits and translates. When you hear it you know that the spirit is still close, and is still interested. Mu nods to the bird as he passes. It flutters its wings and moves off a little. It is not meant to be touched. It is just to let Mu know.

And in the morning Mu is gone.

Part 4: Reframing

I am thinking about Mu, back in my study. Mu and the festival of music, community and spirit. I am sure that not all of what he says is clear, but he is doing, in his own way, what we all do, simply by the fact that we are all here on earth at this time, sharing the space and the situation. He is making his way by striving to make sense and by tuning in to all that is, and being open to joy.

Some things he said I would suggest to qualify. Like this: I accept the idea of all moments coming back to us by the end. But I do not go in search of the past. I think we tend to be bound by past experiences, mostly without knowing how. The practice is to focus on how to live now, to see what binds us and to let go of it. A free person sees possibility in the moment, not the repetition of past patterns.

Occasionally an unexpected thing occurs to remind us of this, like the appearance of a tawny frogmouth owl just near us. I wish to go into the future clean and unencumbered, making new days. The bird is an omen bird. It delivers messages to listeners. This time it says one word: "available".

I am sitting thinking, and the words are being written. At the end the words will say what it is I want them to. There is a need to explore "available". It is the omen word for today. I resort to my old copy of *The Shorter Oxford English Dictionary* to hear the story of this word. It is a great story. The root of the word is value, going back to Middle English, French and Latin. The crux of the story is that it is not just that something is there to be used, but it is useful; it is of value to us.

I enjoyed an American twist on the word, from 1848. A candidate was said to be available if he had a qualification apart from substantial merit that made his success probable. And what was this qualification? It was a lack of "history", what we would call baggage – embarrassing or shameful episodes. So when the

113

owl says "available", it is saying the present is of value to us when we can shed ourselves of the history that weighs us down and holds us back.

Yet I rebel when I hear people say we should "move on" and "leave it behind us". The word "convenient" comes to mind. Invariably when people say this, you can see that it suits their purposes. No great philosophical wisdom is being advocated here. You can easily visualise that they have a past full of shallow graves. What they are proposing is to ignore any possibility of learning how to live better.

I like a saying that is being used in advertising at the moment: "It never gets easier. You just get better." No one gets better from moving on all the time. You just get a longer trail of mistakes you have to leave behind you. Eventually there will be no places left to move to; you will have a history in every one of them. Then, nothing will be available to you.

What is it about, the alternative? This: retrace your path. Return to the source, which is the place where you felt the purity of the original feeling. Feel it again and recover it. The pathways that led away have a myriad of snares – things that happened to you, and things you were responsible for, in weakness or in excess of power, in ignorance or in too much self-assurance. It is all true and it is all unchangeable there, but we unpack the reasons and go behind it, to before it happened, and we learn.

This is the learning, the unpacking of the reasons why we accumulate "history". Next, in the clearing formed by that deconstruction, we can avail ourselves of these words: "Turn and move in the opposite direction from your former path". This gives you ways to realise things. This is the way of returning.

I am coming back to Mu. What is his story? He arrived a long time ago, in a story I wrote when I lived in the valley. He just turned up in a story about a young girl who had endured a difficult childhood. He did not explain himself at the time, he just chanted each day, as a service to the world, to call the world and its people back to the elemental nature of all things. He was stripping away layers of grime, veneers of vanity and delusion.

It was working. Around him people felt less angry, they felt less need to be loud, the sting went out of their attacks on

114

each other. There were changes on more subtle levels too, as if the spirit mother had returned from the mountains to dance at the spring festival and her lightness pervaded the mundane world. Not something to be noticed at large, but suggested by odd things like an owl appearing.

Mu is connected to the spirit world, but his task here is undisclosed. We saw him only briefly as he wandered from place to place chanting, and a girl escaping from cruel parents took on the role of ensuring he would find food and shelter each day. Perhaps he sang her back to sanity and peace.

He comes to mind often, as I wonder what he does after the time of chanting. The festival was the first time he has appeared in many years. It seemed fitting that it was at a music festival he should reappear. He proved to be as enigmatic as before. He might represent the dark animal gods, calling us back to primal powers and unmaking the patterns by which we fool ourselves that we control the world.

It may be that Mu only appears to signify times of great change. Perhaps he was shocked by the stone man because the stone man forgot the past, or wanted to forget, and the task is to remember it, to confront it and redeem it or reconcile yourself to it.

I have tried to say what I think needs to be said about significant events in my past. I have tried to understand what happened. I have not been looking for revenge and I trust I have not wallowed in self-pity or sentimentality. My intention was simply to tell the stories because they needed to be told, to be part of the world's memory. I was not strong enough before, I was too timid when I should have been bold and shouted.

Perhaps. But maybe what happened, in many of those situations, was what was going to happen. The river was flowing that way, taking all with it, and sometimes the only wisdom is knowing when not to speak.

There are other experiences that I have not turned into story. Often, I think it is because those experiences are repetitions. They only happened to see whether I would react the same way, or whether I had actually learned something. Mostly I felt I had learned something and was exercising my experience. Some would say, "What do you do to attract these experiences?" And I say, "Because that is how I learn. How do you learn?"

I am carried forward by the ongoing process of change. It is a process of casting out and drawing back in to digest. From moment to moment it does not seem that I am moving, but I keep in mind the core of an idea, and over time I see how far I have come. But I am not counting goals, I am being grateful that I am connected to the Way. Joy is receptive and expressive, it is not hungry to conquer and dominate. Winning is only winning if the victory is for all of us. If, at the end of the triumph we can all go back to our homes and enjoy meals, conversation and sound sleep, having danced in communion at the spring festival and called up the spirits of new life.

*   *   *   *   *

I am awake in the early morning while a sea of colour pastes the sky. This morning is yellow and orange and later it will be hot. When people rise and dress and get into their cars or wait for buses, they will go to offices and schools and factories and do routine things, although in one place someone will crash their car into the car in front. Somewhere else a manager will come to work in a temper and snap at the first worker he sees.

It will be because the toaster didn't work this morning, or their child was grumpy and wouldn't get ready for school, so they were late and frustrated. It will be because the news has told them, once again, that people in the larger world fight and kill each other. They fight for complex reasons, for survival, or to resist the world view or the gods of other nations, societies and tribes.

I remember Victor Frankl. You don't deal with this by pretending that it does not exist. You have to acknowledge the reality of it and its horror. But nor do you deal with it by allowing it to overwhelm you and lashing out at others, or by losing your concentration and crashing your car into the one in front.

And nor can you deal with it by being agnostic and retreating to the scientific observer pose. Children grow because you love them, not because they are observed rationally. Everything grows and sustains only because enough people maintain the desire to

116

live. And things grow well when people live in harmony with the universe. Then the power of love is greater than all horrors and with perseverance all things return from exile and reconcile.

There are two things in life: principles and circumstance. Neither is enough on its own; both are needed to make a whole. This is the meaning of the yin and yang symbol, that in some places is called the Supreme Ultimate symbol. Things happen, and a person decides how to act in response. There is circumstance, and our actions exhibit principles (whether we think about them or are aware of them or not). This is the yin and the yang.

As Schweitzer said, we make our principles. We are responsible for them. We choose them. It is a thing that humans do. But the foolish think that this makes them masters of the universe. How could you think that when you breathe air you did not make, and eat food that relies on the bounty of the earth? Our ability to decide our principles enables us to create and enjoy, to hold the autumn festival of thanks for the harvest, to build monuments that make us feel wonder, to laugh and surprise each other.

This is not the answer some people want. They want an answer that will guarantee them security and comfort or, if they are thinking of all humanity, they want an answer that will include a system of government, industry and commerce. They want a design for a complete system that will deliver plenty and equity to everyone in a way that is in balance with the earth.

Yes, it is necessary for societies and their leaders to be thinking about systems and governance, and work out how we can all move in this direction. Yes, it is necessary for people in positions of power and influence to be working on the big picture and the longer term, and to keep nudging things in that direction, to be pushing things beyond currently unsatisfactory practices. But a system cannot enable, much less enforce, individuals to live worthwhile lives, or lives that practise positive regard for the well-being of others.

Individually, the threshold is this: you must stand by what you know to be true and find the power to exist independently of collective norms. If you have not taken this stand, it is like being a house whose ridgepole is sagging under a heavy burden. In the end the house will collapse. You need to step out from under the weight of collective norms and determine your own principles as an individual.

This is the great transition, to stand alone without fear. This is to be nourished from within.

∗   ∗   ∗   ∗   ∗

There are more questions. How do I determine my own principles? Isn't it more a case of subscribing to universal principles, like honesty and fairness and caring for others?

I think that the universal principles are the colour palette that you draw from. No one argues about whether or not honesty is a value, or fairness, or caring for others. The question is what they mean in context. That is when you start to paint with the palette. Suppose we talk about the principle of excess. We understand the principle, but what does it mean in practice? Is having two cars excessive, or even having one car?

This is when you start to stand on your own – when you address such issues and accept the idea of becoming clearer about what a principle means in particular contexts, and accept the work of living out the principle so that it is seen in your life. If this is your purpose and your work (that is, you strive to practise the principle), then dross and corruption fall away from you. It is small work like this that accumulates greatness.

It seems slow, like being on a journey when the destination is a long way away. We say, the road is long. We feel melancholy and it is hard to shake it. What is to be said about this? Some people would say, stop feeling sorry for yourself. That is one way. It has its kernel of truth, but if we follow this path we sometimes have to hunt this feeling into a corner and bludgeon it to death. Then we suffer for the crime we have committed.

Or, we turn to humour. We find something funny to laugh at, and discover that our melancholy was not so serious. It shifted, it loosened its hold and scampered away. It was laughable.

But sometimes, the feeling needs to be honoured. Sometimes it is like an artefact half-buried in the ground, and I have dug down to the bottom of it and around it. I have hauled it up to the surface and inspected it. At least then it is something separate

118

from me; it is not me. And I can query where it came from, and what it intends to do with me. Often, it cannot stand the scrutiny and it withers before me.

I would say, contemplate the alternation between fullness and emptiness. There is an aspect of humans that is like tides. We are an ocean with vast depths and a moon above. We are pulled in and out, even as the ships of commerce sail across us on their business. We get caught up being the yin or being the yang when what is best is to focus on the whole. Movements will take their place and it is appropriate to be impressed. Yet the beach knows that the tide will reach its limit and recede.

In the meantime, it is good to forbear, not to do anything out of desperation. It is one thing to feel, it is another thing to act. Sometimes it is best not to do anything at all. And certainly it is best not to make others suffer for what we are feeling. One of the great sadnesses of the tides of melancholy is that some people think it gives them a licence to be cruel and vicious towards others. There is no excuse for this, no excuse.

A long journey? If that were the only truth it would be distressing. There would only be lamentation. But it is also true that the present moment is enough. At all times, whether we choose to feel it or not, we are in the present. The journey and the moment are the yin and the yang. There are two things in life.

What is the principle? Benevolence. It is the only thing that saves you. It is what connects the inner and the outer life.

Is it a question of duty? If I find myself in a certain place, and that place is merely a resting spot in the wilderness, in inhospitable territory, is it duty that sustains me? I might think this about the city, about living in the midst of traffic and a struggling mass of people. Duty might sustain me, duty to contribute to society, duty to be a good citizen, duty to serve an employer. There are manifold duties.

Duty is a welcome master for many people, because it takes care of the job of defining your purpose, and it eliminates the job of questioning the ethics or value of actions. It is a virtue, but it is a secondary virtue. When not qualified it is simply ballast for those who have made decisions about the direction they want things to take. When Hitler decides he wants his society to take a certain shape, the sense of duty of millions of people is simply ballast for his designs. Duty may serve good ends, but it is likewise merely ballast, because it does not produce conscious, informed actions. It simply produces compliance and obedience.

So, duty is useful as a personal tool to bolster perseverance in striving for a goal or in maintaining standards, but it doesn't address the primary question of what goal you will pursue or what principles you will subscribe to, and it is a flawed tool for assessing the ethics of particular actions. Duty is a tool that gangs and crooked organisations use to get their underlings to perpetrate corrupt and evil acts. Following others leads to corruption of the self.

I am weaving a new story. It is time to go forward. It is favourable to cross great rivers. There has been a course of things. I raised a question about the group of which I was a part: is this the right way to act? This set me apart. Then I led a group, and I demonstrated that this was a good way to go about things. But the old ways reasserted themselves, I was crushed and cast out. Later I found a voice, and wrote about how to lead and go about things in a good way. And this did not garner attention, for the most part.

My story of how I led a group was of the effort to be ethical, and the tragedies that destructive people precipitate. It is well-received by a few, but it does not gain traction. I tell another story, of principles in other circumstances. There is no way to present this story to people, so it sits on a shelf. I write again, to talk about the bigger story, of coming to an understanding of principle. In this work, principle is about the yin of society and the yang of business, the articulation of a proper relationship.

Heaven and earth are still moving towards each other. There is a struggle in the outer world and I need barriers, but I work through the receptive. I keep my feet in the earth. The great river is questioning. It is questioning what is duty to the collective. So the boat moves a little way from shore. I am endeavouring to chart my own course. It is a brave act, reasserting principles that I take to be ancient and virtuous. I am audacious, marred only by an excess of passion and a trace of arrogance. I move further from shore and, although sometimes lost, I would never go back

120

to the shore from which I embarked.

Again I question. This time I question myself. I question the simplicity of the answers I felt it necessary to have. I encounter different maps and even different compasses. Different worlds are being charted. It is important to work through the receptive, to let the different layers come into focus. Is it possible for there to be harmonious action? Not always. Sometimes there are mishaps and obstacles. Sometimes it is best to not even try to move forward.

The boat sits in the water and I wonder. I am out of sight of land in all directions. What is different? This: I am not fearful, I am curious and open-minded. And lo, the breeze enters and I am moving. In fact, it is hard to tell when I began to move, because I discover myself moving. What I notice is that the mast is steadfast and upright. I yield to the wind. My way is brilliant and strong. No, it is not my way, it is The Way.

I realise how many misconceptions a statement like this might provoke. It's a pity. The alternative is negative; it is to not ever experience centredness. Would I like to clarify or qualify my statement? I would say, it is about carrying a perspective within you without being attached to it. It is about letting light shine, not making presumptions based on ego attachments to how you might be seen by others.

In the new story, the boat is now gliding across the open water, far from the shore that I started from. And I am sitting in my study, articulating the crossing. The journey is about not staying lost in my experience, but seeing it from multiple, fruitful perspectives. The long aim is to integrate all perspectives, but my immediate aim is much more modest, it is to see this moment from the place where we are all one. This is the great crossing.

I read, "As you move along, your practice incorporates more and more of the pandemonium of the world until, finally and naturally, you practise for your own enlightenment and for the enlightenment of all others as well". That was Ajahn Sumano Bikkhu. It was of interest to me that he frames himself as someone who fled from the city in order to find himself. I loved the idea that our practice "incorporates" the pandemonium of the world. It is like a tiger devouring a bowl of corruption then sitting in calmness.

My experience is that events that occurred that constituted a crisis at the time would be more manageable now. I would understand the events in terms of processes that were occurring, and I would be less fearful about the outcomes. People act out of simple but deep motivations. They want you to acknowledge that they exist and they are of value, they might want you to respect their power or their competence or their devotion, such things. They might play games with you until you let them know that you will not play. And I will not play unless we both know what game we are playing.

We learn. This is the next thing on the journey, to accommodate the idea of learning. What is it I learn, and how do I learn? If there are two things in life, and the two things are learning and living, then learning has to be understood as a counterpoint to living and as something that contributes to better living, not as a substitute for living. Learning is about the goal of becoming all that I can be.

There is an old Beachboys song that tells a tale of the journey of humanity, and it urges that "we should not go down the dinosaurs' way until all of our capacities have been explored". The music intimates that this journey can be wondrous, strong and joyous. What interests me is that there are different types of learning. It is not all the same kind of thing.

There is knowledge of simple facts about ourselves and our surroundings – knowing how tall you are, knowing how long it takes to walk to the local shops. And knowing processes – how to open a door or dress ourselves. Then there is more exquisite intellectual knowledge – being able to explain photosynthesis or how a car works. There is knowledge about people and emotions – knowing that the child is in a good mood, or knowing that the boss is upset about something, even knowing how we ourselves are feeling, and why.

This is only the beginning. There are many, many types of knowing, and reading books or listening to teachers only gets you there some of the time. For much of it, we have to experience things and process them through reflection, and the learning is not certain, and nor is it confirmed by an external authority.

122

This is the crux of our personal dilemma. The learning we need in order to relate meaningfully to another person is subtle and nuanced, and very seldom can someone else tell us authoritatively what is right, or effective.

You probably know this. You have probably been in a situation where two people are agitating each other and their voices get louder as their feelings begin to spiral out of control. And you know exactly what each person is thinking and you could stop it all right now if they would both listen to you. But they wouldn't and you know this so you say nothing. You let it take its course.

Well, at least we can learn to know ourselves better, so we don't have to be either of those two people. So the authority for our learning is our experience, not just our own doings, but also our observations of others. But you have to think about the experiences, you have to remember them, and think what people's motivations might be for their behaviour.

I know that masters of their trade or profession always give themselves time after a job or a project to go over it again in their mind, to think of every aspect of it they can remember. They retrace their steps, and think about parts they could have done better, or parts they were very pleased with. This is the real stuff, sifting and salvaging, and storing both the good solutions and the risks to be aware of when they are doing the next project. This is the vital work, the learning. This is when the master is at his/her finest.

*　　*　　*　　*　　*

It is said that the story unfolds. Here is an example. I went shopping for shoes, and it became a story. It was a simple quest: to buy ordinary black shoes that one wears to an office. I decided it would be good to buy them from a shoe shop rather than a department store, because it is a good thing that shoe shops exist, and the people there probably care about shoes and customer service.

When I got them out of the box at home, I saw that the eyelet on one of the shoe lace holes was torn or cut, so I took the shoes back to the shop. This is the story that unfolded. When I showed the fault to the shop assistant she first said, "That's very unusual".

I wasn't sure if she was implying anything by this remark. Did she mean, "That's unusual", or was she implying that the unusual occurrence was the fault of the shopper? So I waited to see if there would be further clarification. None came.

Then, very quickly, she said, "A lot of these shoes were on special because they had imperfections". Now this was a lie, because when I bought the shoes, there was no evidence that this was the case – no sign saying "Damaged shoes for sale", no warning from the shop assistant about the possible state of the shoes, no such thing. Just a sign to say "Special price" (although as you might guess, not so very special).

I didn't feel that I should respond to this statement, given that I would have to be impolite and accuse the shop assistant of lying to me. So I waited to see what she would do next. As yet, she had said nothing about what she was going to do about the damaged shoe.

When she realised that she was going to have to respond to me by suggesting some action that she would take, she said she would go out the back and see if there was a replacement shoe. I thought this was a reasonable suggestion and indicated as such to her.

It turned out that there wasn't a replacement shoe in that size. Instead of the size 8½ shoe which I had bought, she offered me a size 8. I couldn't see what I would want with a size 8 shoe when I had bought a size 8½ shoe, so I said "No, thank you".

Her next offer was that she could send away for a replacement shoe. I imagined a series of phone calls, couriers, lost orders, loading docks and ocean liners, and weeks and weeks of leaves torn out of desktop calendars. I would be going to the office barefoot for the foreseeable future. I needed shoes today. So I said "No, thank you".

With her first suggestion of panic, she said, "Would you like to pick out another pair of shoes in the shop?"

But I had been in this shop a couple of days previously, examining the range of shoes there, and I had chosen the ones I had bought. Not any of the others. So I said, "No, thank you, I do not want any other shoes."

124

The truth was, I didn't want to buy shoes from a shop assistant who started the conversation by leaving open the implication that I had damaged the shoes, and who had then compounded that insult by suggesting that I had knowingly bought damaged shoes and subsequently had the hide to complain that they were damaged.

There were no further options to be explored, but it was still necessary for me to say, "I would like a refund, please".

She didn't actually ask me if I would like a refund. Or perhaps I didn't wait long enough. Perhaps she would have arrived at that conclusion, given enough time. But by then I figured she was unlikely to get there very quickly, and I needed to go and shop for shoes.

What did it end up being a story about? For me, it was about not getting drawn into the argument that the shop assistant wanted to have, and not feeling obliged to accept the unsatisfactory solutions that she was offering me so as to avoid dealing with the essential problem. I realised that I didn't have to argue, all I had to do was let her play out all her avoidance strategies until there was nothing left for her to do but give me a refund.

Nor did I have to lecture her on how she should do her job. That was her business. She was at liberty to realise afterwards that all her strategies had failed and she had been forced to give the customer a refund. She couldn't have argued to herself that what had eventually transpired had been unjust. And if she has been waiting for me to come back to buy more shoes then she will have noticed that her wait has been in vain.

I heard that at a huge retail sale, people clawed their way over each other to get to the stalls that had bargains on them, crushing each other for the promise of saving a few dollars on the purchase of some consumer goods – clothes, mobile phones, shoes, who knows? And a man pulled a gun on another man so that he could buy the last mobile phone on sale. He didn't intend to steal the mobile phone, he just wanted to be the one to buy it, to save a few dollars.

There is madness afoot, and it is collective; people share in it. I would say the lesson here is, there is no need to fight. There is no need to fight for bargains, refunds or shoes. And because the madness is collective, the first thing you have to do is separate yourself from it. I would say "disentangling". That is the word I like. It is the capacity to distinguish between things – to accept and reject. Then you can go on your way unperturbed.

Lose your entanglements. Let go of things. Strip away the layers. Decrease. Make an offering to emptiness.

*   *   *   *   *

I have tried to stop moving. Time goes so fast if you let it. We have so many important things to do, everything is so urgent. This is what people say. But I wonder what they do? Do they schedule their days from wake until sleep? Do they keep to the schedule? What delays them? What happens to tasks that remain undone, at the end of a day, at the end of a week?

In practice, tasks and appointments seldom fit neatly into the slots we have allocated to them. One task that you thought would take an hour takes half a day. Another task that was going to take two hours is resolved in five minutes. An appointment you had scheduled doesn't happen because the person got sick, so you finished two other tasks instead.

Or, your body took a holiday for a day. Instead of finishing the task that has been waiting for a week, you spent the time filing papers because you were sick of your desk being so cluttered. You feel guilty about the unfinished task, but you don't enjoy doing it anyway.

The great fear is, if you stop running, everything will start to unravel. You will spiral down into the pit, you will fall like Alice into Wonderland. If we don't have enough time, we don't have enough of anything, because everything occurs in time – money, achievements, relationships.

I am still learning time. I am a beginner. It still tries to fool me and intimidate me. It still likes to pretend that time is about blocks and how they fit into a grid. And on this model, I am always deficient. I have too many blocks and not enough spaces in the grid.

But, suppose time is about spirit, and this is largely about relationships? Then the thing to watch is how my use of time affects relationships. Perhaps there is a natural limit to the number and extent of relationships I can maintain. It's also about keeping my word. If I promised a job to someone by a certain time, then keeping my word is honouring the relationship. If I have to defer, I should communicate with the person and perhaps explain why it won't happen by then, and when it will happen.

In practice there are myriads of variations on how I handle it. But I start with the concept of relationship and I try to keep my word, because relationships are built on trust and reliability. This is tough, and it means having to periodically reassess what it is reasonably possible for me to do. It means reassessing my passion as well, and realising when I should drop something.

It's still hard to be true to myself. I like Oriah Mountain Dreamer's words in "The Invitation" when she says you have to be prepared to disappoint another in order to be true to yourself. There is deep truth in this. It seems that, today, so many of us try to extend ourselves to cover too many activities, trying to "keep up" with work, family, professional development, friends, recreation, community and networks.

I remember Mu and the girl singer at the music festival: "Thank you for giving me your attention". If time is about relationships, then our attention is a gift that we give to someone or something, and it generates joy or peace, something like that. Perhaps it is that we are creating opportunities for gratitude.

And it's important who we give our attention to. Instead, our minds are running down a dark corridor, looking this way and that like Alice, trying to see someone who will give us the kind of attention we want, if we even knew what that was.

When I examine this, I unearth things about myself. Why do I give my attention to this thing? Ah, it is because I feel the need to keep in touch with a certain network. And why is that? Ah, because I am uncertain about my professional identity. Oh, and why is that a concern? What is my fear? What is my passion and interest?

You see, it helps. Our use of time is about where we put our energy, and that is about the relationships we wish to establish or maintain. Once we start to unpick the web we have woven around ourselves, we can see, perhaps uncomfortably, that we have choices, and we can change those choices.

I look at this from two perspectives. One is a rational view. If you are continually flustered, and continually running from one thing to another, and you don't seem to be enjoying it, you need to make some rational choices about what you can manage and still stay sane.

But there is also a spirit perspective. If the running is grinding you down, where are you running to? When do you expect to get there? And what will change then? Will you be happy? If your spirit were something you were responsible for looking after, how does it feel now? Is it joyful about all the great things you are doing? Does it rejoice daily in all your wonderful relationships, and how you sustain them constantly?

Life doesn't have to be easy, but it has to nourish the spirit. You can be busy, but it has to be something that your spirit thinks is worthwhile being devoted to. The spirit understands devotion better than it understands logic.

It turns out that our handling of time is in fact about happiness. A psychologist of the 1930s, W. Beran Wolfe, wrote a neat piece about happiness that shows how it connects with our use of time:

> If you observe a really happy man you will find him building a boat, writing a symphony, educating his son, growing double dahlias in his garden, or looking for dinosaur eggs in the Gobi desert. He will not be searching for happiness as if it were a collar button that has rolled under the radiator. He will not be striving for it as a goal in itself. He will have become aware that he is happy in the course of living life twenty-four crowded hours of the day.

I make the assumption that happiness is not achieved directly. Rather, it is an attribute of the person who lives well. I read *Sons and lovers* (D.H. Lawrence) when I was sixteen and never forgot the words of Paul Morel, when he was asked if he were happy: "So long as life's full, it doesn't matter whether it's happy or not." (I am also willing to admit that Paul was feeling perverse

128

at the time.) This may explain why the only time I would doubt my happiness is when people ask me if I am happy.

*   *   *   *   *

The story goes on and I try to be a master by doing less and doing it more consciously. I write and it is like cooking an offering for the ancestors. It is a slow business most of the time, but in tending the cooking vessel I have put ghosts to rest and watched the aromas rise. I observe how things take shape in situations and what there is to learn about virtue and efficacy in those situations. There is a tension in situations between our experience and the ideas we bring to it. With different ideas we have different experiences and therefore take different actions.

I have to address the question of differing accounts of situations. My story of an event might be different from another person's, and the two versions may conflict. What does this mean? Some people who write about stories say that they are eternally contestable and revisable; this is the nature of things. This is like the detective who comes along with new evidence that puts the original conclusion in doubt, or the historian who re-examines history from a feminist viewpoint.

This seems problematic, but if we paint a scenario for the detective example, using the new evidence the detective retraces all aspects of the crime and follows the new leads. The result is that the original conclusion is revised but, and this is the point, we are now satisfied that we have a satisfactory explanation for what happened. The case is closed.

In some possible future we may find that everyone involved in the crime was a participant in an elaborate charade and everything we had concluded about the crime is wrong. Nevertheless, sanity is maintained by assuming that we have now got the story essentially right. Even if we have to acknowledge the theoretical possibility that it could all still be different. At this point it is just an intellectual quibble and our attention might be better gifted elsewhere.

A different issue is if my stories are the result of my biases and blindnesses, particularly if they are self-serving. If I am a liar or I am covering up something significant, then that is one thing. But the answer to this is simple. I may be found out and then my trust with the reader is broken and my stories unravel. No one will believe what I say from then on.

This has happened to writers who have purported through their books to be something they are not. Even if the writing is good, readers generally object to being fooled in this way and withdraw their loyalty. There is another circumstance too, where a writer presents him/herself as a certain type of person through their books, and then, in real life, they act in a way that violates that implicit pact. This too is generally fatal to their future writing projects.

However, mostly this argument is about bias. It is to say that the story would look very different if I hadn't been so dismissive of a certain character or circumstance, for example. Or, what would the story look like from another character's point of view?

My answer is to say I didn't set out to represent all points of view or everything that happened. And if I exhibited biases, then that is how it was at the time, in the story. My only wish was that the reader might gain some insights into my experience and think about the challenges that arise in seeking to be an ethical leader. I still feel that I have done this well, and I am still trying to learn and develop along that path.

I think this leads to the question, when is a story "finished", meaning, when has it reached the point that it presents a story completely enough and coherently enough and with a clear-enough point? All of these criteria are qualitative, of course, and different people will have different definitions of the criteria and different opinions on whether the criteria have been met in a particular work. Well, in conversation we hope to reach some common understanding and agreement about these things.

What about the question? I say, for me, it has to feel complete. It has to answer the central questions that have been raised as the story unfolds. In the shoe story above, the question is simple: there is a new pair of shoes where one has been found to be damaged. What will happen? Then, as I enter the shop and encounter the shop assistant's attitude, how will it get resolved? How will I deal with the shop assistant?

The point for me in this story is the choices I had in responding to the shop assistant's behaviour, all the common responses people make to such a situation. I could have shouted and remonstrated, I could have been sarcastic, I could have threatened to bring in the government regulator. I felt I didn't need to say anything about these choices, because we all know it. They are common, even archetypal, in our consumer culture.

So the story was complete when the shop assistant had run out of inappropriate responses. My point is that when there is only one inevitable outcome in a situation (unless I had drawn a gun and demanded a refund), sometimes you only have to let things run their course. Of course you have the choice of short-circuiting the process at any stage, if you run out of patience, for example. Perhaps we should all carry a gun.

I can reveal, at this point, that I did find new shoes. I went to a department store, where I found a nice range of choices and selected a suitable pair. You will want to know what the customer service was like. Disappointingly, it was very poor. The store was under-staffed and it was far too long before I was able to capture a shop assistant's attention.

So it seems that, after all this, the central issue is having enough time and knowing what to do with our attention. At least this shop assistant was polite, just a little harried.

It is harder to say when bigger stories are complete. It doesn't matter so much. It is not as if you are presenting half of a mathematical equation. It is more indefinable. It is like asking when is a painting finished, or when is the cooking complete? My rule is that it has to make sense, at least to me, and/or it has to be enjoyable.

And then there is the returning, from the process to stillness again. Here is an image of that returning.

I sit within the midst of the six omens:

There is thinking and
there is feeling,
there is the past and
there is the future,
there is the earth (the material world), and

there is heaven (spirit).
I return to awareness of the one
which is all that is.

I am not yet done with the story of stories. It does not feel complete or satisfactory. I can live, but I still wonder what I can do with stories. I come back to the fragmentation of stories in our culture. Stories in ancient time told us about the sun and the moon and the earth and the sky, and how they got here, and how we got here. Then these stories were taken over by science.

Those stories were exciting too. When Galileo asserted that the earth was not the centre of the universe, but earth was simply one of several planets that revolved around a sun in a distant corner of a galaxy, this must have been extraordinary. And when the Pope excommunicated him from the church for his "beliefs", and how the proposition was eventually accepted as true, that is a great story.

But the old stories then became merely quaint. I am not trying to bring them back. What I want to extract from them is an essence. Those stories are not about science any more. There is no need for them in that way. But what the stories also say is that there is a sense in which our lives have meaning and it matters how we live our lives. As Victor Frankl said, it matters how we live our lives. This is not for the sake of a creed or a doctrinal belief system, but because we are humans here altogether, conscious of ourselves and each other, and affected by whether we are cruel or kind to each other. And we look out and within to things that are deep and of which we are only dimly aware.

It is the power of stories to take us along a path, to allow us to enter into an experience that we use to enlarge our vision of life and our feeling for it. I see this going back to the stories I used to read my children, seeing what they enjoyed and imagining what a story might mean to their young minds. Now that I have grandchildren, the same stories go on – *Scuffy the Tugboat, Where the Wild Things Are, The Very Hungry Caterpillar, Are You My Mother?* (There are lots.)

Later, for me and some of my children too, there were fantasy and science fiction books, which went further and painted worlds in which stories happened. And these stories made us think about life too, our lives and societies, and their beliefs and norms. The stories tell us that this society we live in is not the only one possible. It could be different, and in realising this, we know that it could be better or worse and there are choices involved.

When we have the notion of story, we can come to human behaviour and see it as a story, as one instance of many possible stories. The mappers among us try to map frameworks of all the possible stories and then explain the relationships between them, the factors that lead to one story rather than another. The psychiatrist Eric Berne wrote about life scripts (*What do you say after you say hello?*), maintaining that people tend to fit their lives into a script, and he mapped a number of kinds of scripts. There are tragic scripts, hero scripts, victim scripts, clever scripts, perseverance scripts, and so on. For example, a girl projects the image of "I'm a cute kid" but there is a sub-text of "but I'm an orphan".

But most of us are buried in a particular story and cannot see the way out. I say, a good life requires us to come out of the stories we are inside of, and live life as an adult. It is not a question of being free of stories, but our stories can get better, which is to say we can free ourselves of the stories that bind us and prevent us from being all that we may be. We can choose to define ourselves by stories that make our life worth living.

The wandering sage sojourns in the shadow lands to find the new connection.

If I find my experience is oppressive because I got hurt or was cheated, I say, this is the omen of the past. Dig it up, put it there on the ground where we can see it, and let's look at it from another side.

That is me sitting there, between the omen of the past and the omen of the future. I sit between them, which is to say it is I who can stop the future from looking like the past. The tiger devours the past and makes room for the new.

I remember, I asked the tiger spirit, "What is the story I should tell now?" and I have my answer. The story is about how to make a new story, but one that honours the ancients. It is not an arrogant story of masters of the universe. It is about understanding the vital bonds between joy and correctness. It is about tuning into all that is present, being grateful for it and adding to the love that is in the world.

For this we must learn poetry, art, music and dance, because the understanding comes through metaphor and through bodily feeling. And it requires awareness, for example, awareness of when we are filling up and we need to empty ourselves so we can listen and see and sense the hearts of other people. It requires an open heart, laughter and play. It requires the disarming of fear.

What would the sage say, when he comes back from the shadow lands? How would he articulate the crossing and the new connection? I am afraid that the sage will say, "I cannot tell you. It would not make any sense to you. You must go yourself." Then I would wonder whether there is any point. Perhaps the sage is a fraudster.

I remember, "We would be creators". Yes, we must live in harmony with ourselves and other species. May tawny frogmouth owls always be around to land on a nearby tree, but what are we to do with our urge to be striving?

I wrote this about writing:

I urge to write.
I am wonder why
this sometimes crude flush of words.

It was odd the way it came out in an ungrammatical rush, like a baby foal being born, that lands on the ground with legs sprawling everywhere. But alive and full of potential ("wild hoping", Bonnie Raitt called it in a song). So when I talk about practice, the point of practice is to get ourselves to be present, so that we may be aware of the full extent of the moment, and be free to be a creator.

The cautious would remind me that creation can be for good or evil. But not for you, not if you have understood the bond between joy and correctness, how they are inextricably linked, like archetypal lovers, like heaven and earth.

What does the sage say? Does he bring a story?

The sage reminds me it was I who said, "Each our own way we must go to the desert, where the angels will minister to us".

134

But the sage does have something to say. He tells this story, or rather, he gives us a metaphor and asks us to consider our relationship to it.

A man left the settled world to build a house at the borders. He was surrounded by the ghosts of the past and the angry mayhem of the outcasts. He learned that the wilderness is dangerous. He was bailed up in his house and threatened by a crew of the outcasts, who were desperate enough perhaps to kill him. He survived through a combination of boldness and cunning. When they wanted to beat him with clubs he stood up to them with thunder in his voice and they backed down, but he needed cunning too to escape.

The sage says, "Establish households. Consider your relationships within the household. You each have a part to play in it, and together you make the unit. It functions well when you play your part and respect the part of others, and you give yourself to the order of the household."

The sage says, "There are two hosts in the household, man and woman."

And I take him to be saying, there is not one who dominates the other, but two people who work for the whole and who seek to complement each other. And this is only achieved through self-examination and correcting continually.

I apply the metaphor to the self as well. So I come back to joy and correctness, yin and yang, balance. They are my two hosts. So my goal is to know what is created when they are both honoured in the self. It is as strong as a household.

The sage also says this: "Be substantial in your words and consistent in your deeds".

This is understated but pungent. To be substantial in my words I must say what I stand for. I can't get away with saying nothing. I have to make a stand. And then, having said it, I have to live up to it. If I say I value caring for others, I have to do that, I have to be that.

Is the sage done? This is a good story. It is enough to go on with for now.

But there is one more thing. The sage says, "Consider that the story is already fulfilled. You have crossed the great river and set things right. Light and water pass through the primal gate and unite. You are on your way to the spring festival. What now? Everything is in its place. You are surrounded by danger but you are secure within."

What, then?

"The situation requires care and attention. You go on with what you are doing, but the moon has waxed and it will wane. Adapt to what crosses your path, give help to others, remain steadfast and upright. Thus the energy flows in all directions. Stay open to the spirits and remember, you do not need to force things to completion. Indeed, that will bring you undone. Take preventive measures against decline."

So, it is like this, after all that. The story goes on and I try to be a master by doing less and doing it more consciously. I make offerings to the ancestors to keep alive my connection to ancient virtue.

It is a slow business most of the time, but in tending the cooking vessel I have put ghosts to rest and watched the aromas rise.

The flying words cross the boundary of death to bring new life.

*   *   *   *   *

ORDER FORM

✉ **Order by email:** info@glennmartin.com.au

💻 **Order from website:** www.glennmartin.com.au

✉ **Order by post:** G.P. Martin Publishing
5 Gumnut Place, Cherrybrook NSW 2126 AUSTRALIA

☎ **Order by fax:** 61 (0)2 9945 0524

Please send me prices + postage on the following books by Glenn Martin:

Book	Quantity
The Big Story Falls Apart	
To the Bush and Back to Business	
The Ten Thousand Things: A story of the lived experience of the I Ching	
Sustenance	
Human Values and Ethics in the Workplace	
The Little Book of Ethics: A human values approach	
Flames in the Open	
Love and Armour	

Discounts available for bookshops and wholesale purchasers.

Name: ....

Address: ....

....

Town/city: ....

Country: .... ZIP/Postcode: ....

Phone: .... Mobile: ....

email: ....

www.ingramcontent.com/pod-product-compliance
Lightning Source LLC
Chambersburg PA
CBHW030336020726
47493CB00004B/1295